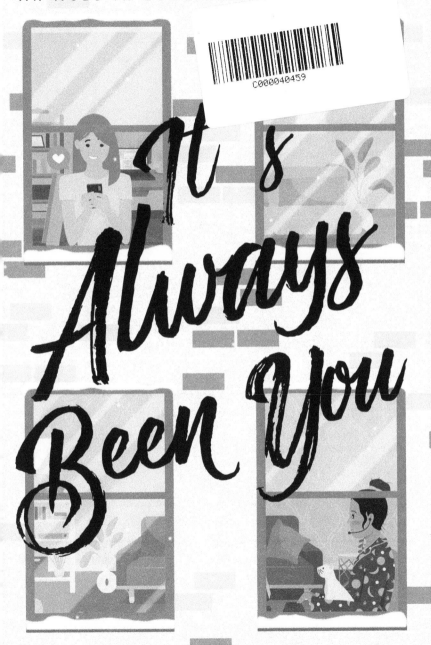

It's Always Been You

ELIN ANNALISE

First published in April 2021 by Ineja Press

Cover Design by Sarah Anderson Designs
Interior Formatting by Sarah Anderson Designs

Paperback ISBN: 978-1-912369-32-4
eBook ISBN: 978-1-912369-31-7

The author can be contacted via email at ElinAnnalise@outlook.com

ELIN ANNALISE

It's Always Been You

INEJA PRESS

ONE
Courtney

"I AM HAVING the worst day ever." My voice is flat as I stare at the mess in front of me. Broken ceramic pieces litter the worktop. The newly opened carton of milk is on its side, and its contents is still dripping down the counter and onto the floor.

"Just chill," Dylan says, because of course he does—that's his catch phrase. "Seriously, you always over-react to everything." His voice is tinny in my left ear.

My phone's in my pocket, and the tangled earphones only just reach my jaw, let alone my ear, and every now and then I try to stretch too far, only to have my head yanked back down. No wonder my neck's aching.

"No, you don't understand." I stare at the mess. "It's that damn cat again." It has to be. Sergeant Ginger Paws must've got in here. I mean, don't even get me started on the name—the cat isn't doesn't even have ginger paws, he's just pure white. His name makes no sense. Last time he got into my apartment, he broke my favorite mug and bowl—presents from Zoe and Zara for my twenty-first birthday—and then knocked over the milk. Plus, because of all the panic-buying going on at the supermarkets due to the snow, the only place I could get milk was the expensive corner shop. But, seriously, four quid for a carton of milk I won't be able to drink? Great.

Dylan laughs softly. "You love that cat, really."

"I most definitely do *not*. He's not even mine—Mrs. Dalton should keep better control of him than this." I freeze as I remember last week's shenanigans and how Mrs. Dalton told me Sergeant Ginger Paws has a weak stomach. "He better not have drunk any of the milk," I mutter, looking around for him. Is he still in my apartment?

A cat having diarrhea all over my bed is about the only way this day could get any worse. First, it was my laptop breaking this morning—when I dropped a stack of hardcovers on it— then it was me realizing that while I now had milk, I'd forgotten to buy my favorite cereal, *and* that I'd forgotten to spend my Marks & Spencer vouchers before they expired.

I breathe out slowly. I need to find Sergeant Ginger Paws.

Ever since the Daltons moved in with their zoo, their animals have been trying to take over my home. Before the cat began his regular visits, I found one of their budgies flying around my kitchen. Eventually, Mrs. Dalton came and collected 'precious Arthur.'

"Courtney, just chill." Dylan is laughing—I can tell by the way his words flutter. "You just need to have a more positive attitude."

"Yeah, because that will fix everything," I mutter, quickly collecting the broken pieces of the mug and bowl. I toss them in the bin—I don't need the damn cat hurting himself and leaking blood everywhere as well while I'm trying to find him, even if it would provide a trail for me to follow. "What I need is a drink." Preferably a whole bottle of wine.

Only then I remember I promised Mum I'd go the whole of January without touching a drop. I roll my eyes. As if I need to prove that I'm not an alcoholic! Well, she's going to have to take back that accusation when I manage Dry January easily.

I do a quick walkthrough of my apartment—the whole thing's open plan, and the bedroom and bathroom are the only 'rooms' of sorts. Those doors are shut and have been for hours, so if Sergeant Ginger Paws is still in here he's got to be in the living/kitchen area.

And there's no sound nor sight of the cat.

Dylan laughs. "Just be calmer about everything. Honestly, it works. It's all about mindset." As he drones on and on about the benefits of meditation, I tune out his words. I've heard them all before because if there's one thing Dylan likes talking about, it's meditation.

There's a reason why he teaches it, even if his students do expect more of a relaxing class than a lecture. That's how Dylan and I met. Shortly after university, I joined his class. The two of us hit it off instantly, and we've been good friends ever since.

I trip over my laundry basket just outside the bathroom as I search for the cat and nearly end up headbutting the wall. I let out a frustrated cry, then scoop up the basket. May as well load this into the washing machine and start it.

"And that's exactly why you *should*," Dylan says.

"Mmhmm." I stride across the kitchen. The washing machine is under the countertop, but I don't think any milk has gone on it. Thank God. I hate cleaning up milk spillages—and if you don't quite get rid of it all, it gives the whole area a sour smell.

"Courtney? You're not listening to a word I say."

"No, I *am*." I shove the laundry into the machine, tip some bio gel into the measuring cup and toss that in too—and the movement wrenches out my earphone. It clangs against the counter, and I scramble to put it back in.

"Oh my God, Court! Can't you just sit and relax when we talk? You know, catch-ups are supposed to be fun and nice." Dylan sounds mildly annoyed now. "I can tell you're still doing chores. Next it'll be the vacuuming."

I roll my eyes. "It's called multi-tasking. And I'm at the center later, so I've got to get as much done now as I can."

I start the washing machine, and it makes a creaking sound as the drum turns. I hold my breath, waiting for smoke or something bad to happen, but fortunately nothing does, and the creaking stops. Just the machine acting normally. I breathe a sigh of relief.

"Anyway, I'm getting Kayla later," Dylan says. "She's staying the whole weekend at mine for once. Want to join us for ice cream in the park tomorrow morning?"

"Sure," I say.

"Good." He's smiling again, I'm positive of that. "And we can plan my birthday party."

I hold up my hand, even though he can't see it. "You mean, *I* can plan your party. You can't plan your own one."

Dylan laughs. "Just nothing too wild."

"*Nothing Too Wild* is my middle name," I say. "And my brand. It's totally my brand."

I am famous for throwing parties. Ever since I was thirteen and got away with organizing an awesome midnight party—complete with a freaking chocolate fountain—that the teachers had no idea about at our boarding school, my friends called me the Party Queen. That name followed me from St. Bridget's Academy for Girls to Edinburgh University, where I studied for a BA in Interior Design, and my parties became more sophisticated. The Party Queen is still who I am. Because I throw great parties. Fun ones, quirky ones, weird ones. You name it, I can do it.

And I know just the thing for Dylan. Already, I'm smiling widely. Thinking about party planning lightens my mood. "You're not going to regret this," I say, because since when has anyone regretted a party organized by Courtney Davenport? No one. That's who.

"I mean it," Dylan says. "I'll be a respectable man of twenty-eight. And I don't want a repeat of last year."

"Well last year it was your mum behind all the party planning. Not me."

His mum had thrown him a dinosaur-themed party. Well, okay, it was meant for Dylan's daughter, Kayla, obviously, as the two of them have their birthdays only days apart. Dylan's is on the eighth, and Kayla's on the eleventh. Dylan's mum had booked out the whole play center for Kayla, only at the last minute Kayla's mum had returned. She had taken Kayla away on a long weekend, knowing there was nothing Dylan could do about it. We actually managed to rebook Kayla's party for the following week at Dinosaur World and updated the parents of all her friends on this, but when we'd tried to cancel the original booking for the eleventh, the manager told us it was non-refundable. Rather than cancelling and losing all the money, Dylan's mum had had the great idea that Dylan's birthday could be celebrated that day instead. The looks on the workers' faces were priceless when they saw who the birthday 'child' was.

The party had had a good turnout too. Zoe and Zara dropped by, as did many regulars from Dylan's meditation group and a couple of his old university friends. Even Dylan's on-again off-again boyfriend Jack had managed to drop in—though I don't think any of us had been quite sure whether they were currently off or on.

But a bunch of adults charging around Dinosaur World? Well, once you got over the cringy nature of it, it had been quite fun. Until Zoe had got stuck in the vertical foam rollers that led to the ball bit. We'd all been trying to push and pull her through—and eventually she'd made it (albeit cursing about how her cleavage was clearly the part of her body causing the trouble), but when she'd suddenly launched into the ball pit, she'd landed on Zara, her twin. They'd both ended up with bloody noses.

"Don't worry, this isn't a joint party for you and Kayla," I tell Dylan. "We'll do something separate for her birthday as well." I head into my bedroom, closing the door quickly behind me in case Sergeant Ginger Paws *is* still about, and look in my wardrobe.

Yes. It's still there. An idea's forming already.

I smile, and Dylan goes on and on about the new dollhouse he's bought for his daughter.

"Can you believe it? It has actual working taps. And a whole plumbing system. I mean, it should do for the price. Eight hundred quid."

"Eight hundred?" I let out a low whistle and head back into the main area of my apartment and—

I stare at the water pouring out of the washing machine. The whole of the kitchen floor is wet.

I rush forward, making a half-strangled sound as I get wet socks.

"Courtney?"

"The washing machine is flooding my kitchen now," I pant, turning it off on the wall. My feet splash about in the water. It's warm. I was doing a forty-degree wash.

I've been having trouble with this machine for a few months, which Dylan knows all about.

First, the water stopped pouring into the machine at its usual rate and the not-enough-water alarm would go off. I solved that by unblocking the inlet pipe. So, that was fine.

But then the fabric conditioner stopped being automatically added during the last rinse of the cycle. Problem solved by pouring it through the drawer and washing it down with a bit of water manually, at the right time.

"Mate, just get a new machine." Dylan says.

The thing about Dylan is that he's from old money. Just like almost everyone at St. Bridget's and a good proportion of those I met at university. And although I have more money now, I remember what it was like to have none. That way of life was so deeply ingrained in me, that I still follow those rules. I've got some savings in my bank account, but they're for emergencies. For unexpected bills. And while you could say needing a new washing machine *is* an unexpected bill, I also have this desire to just try and fix it.

I fixed the oven when it stopped heating up. I looked up what the problem could be, and by a process of deduction and elimination, worked out it was the element. I ordered the new one and watched YouTube videos on how to change it. A week later, and I had a working oven, a new appreciation for the machine, and it had only cost me twenty pounds or so.

So *of course* I'm going to try and repair the washing machine. Buying a new one is a last resort. And, besides, I like finding out how things work. I like the challenge of trying to fix something even if it seems absolutely impossible.

Mum always says fixing things is character building.

"I'll have to call you back later," I say to Dylan. "This thing needs my full attention."

For several moments after our call disconnects, I just stand in the water, staring at the machine, weighing up my options for what I should do right this moment. It's got to be the door seal, that much I'm sure of.

So, I need a new door seal.

But what about my clothes inside? They'll be nowhere near washed, soaking and soapy. I try the door, but of course it's still locked shut. Probably a good thing too else I'd have unleashed way more water across my floor.

I take a deep breath. A quick turn of the dial, a flick of the power switch, and the machine drains—with more water going over my floor.

Oh well. I ignore it. Going to have to mop the floor anyway.

Once the drain cycle has finished and the doors have unlocked, I open the door and drag out sopping wet clothes and throw them into a shopping bag—one of those big sturdy ones with canvas handles. There's a washing machine at the center. I'll put the load on there, and by the time I've finished my shift, there'll be a nice load of damp laundry waiting for me to bring home. Then I can chuck it all in the drying pod that's in my room.

Lifting the canvas bag nearly breaks my back. "Holy sheep," I mutter. I'm still in the habit of not actually swearing, thanks to being around Dylan's daughter for so long. He and I came up with a long list of alternatives and they really have stuck. Causes quite the laugh when I say one of them at work though.

The clock chimes, and I stare at it on the kitchen wall for a moment. How is it that time already?

Hurriedly, I gather my things, the bag of wet laundry, and head to the front door. I pull on my thickest coat—because it's still like the Arctic outside—and then search for my snow boots. What? They're not here. I frown. Where the hell did I leave them? A quick search does not produce them, so I pull on the ballet pumps that are by the door. Not ideal footwear for snow and ice.

The corridor outside smells a little musty, and I wrestle with the bag which seems to have about doubled in weight.

Just as I'm about to open the outer door and leave Hawklands—the block where I live—Mrs. Dalton, my neighbor and the owner of Sergeant Ginger Paws and a myriad of other animals, catches me.

"Ah, Courtney." Mrs. Dalton has big curly hair that always looks like it could do with a brush. Apparently, she pays a lot of money to maintain it like that. She smiles widely at me, revealing perfect teeth. "Just a word of warning, but tomorrow morning my step-daughter is moving in. She's got a lot of stuff, and the van is gonna be out here for a while, I think. I'm afraid it'll block your window again."

"It's fine," I say. But it's nice that she's concerned about it.

"Bless her," Mrs. Dalton says. "She doesn't want to move back. Was adamant that she could manage. Poor Fifi."

Fifi? I raise my eyebrows. What a name. Then I realize Mrs. Dalton is staring at me. "Well, thanks for letting me know," I say, huffing as I readjust my laundry bag. At this rate, I won't ever need to join the gym. And oh my God—the washing better not freeze. I mean, could it? Surely it's cold enough? Frozen clothes are really not what I want.

I manhandle the laundry through the doorway, to the end of the road, and onto the bus. For once, I've timed my outings right, and I get to the stop just as the bus does, despite how slow I am. Luckily the pavements aren't too icy—they've actually been gritted—but carrying sopping wet washing really slows you down. Why the hell didn't I wring out my clothes first? Could've probably squeezed half the River Exe down my sink.

I sit downstairs, on the bus, in the middle. My laundry bag's on the floor next to me, and I'm panting like a loon. Wait, is that PC to think that? I don't think it is, and I feel my face flush as if I've been told off.

At work, Sally and I are doing this project about calling out offensive and insensitive terms. I thought it would be easy, but after we began doing research and really thinking about everything critically, it turns out problematic words are ingrained in so much of society. And in me. I make a mental note to come up with a better simile.

The bus rumbles off, and I put in my earphones and navigate to my latest playlist. The music sweeps me away for five minutes, ten minutes, fifteen, and I find myself thinking about what I might want for my next tattoo. I've got a bumble bee on the back of my neck, and roses down my right thigh. There's a bracelet of stars around my left ankle and—

Cold water seeps into my shoes.

I startle and look down. My eyes widen as I see the water running there—rivulets of it, slipping over my ballet pumps.

Oh my God. My washing. I lift up one side of the laundry bag, and the movement unleashes a torrent of cold water. I yelp as more gets my foot. It's icy cold now.

Then I look forward.

The bus is still pretty empty—but I see a woman in the seats near the front. See her two young children, both of whom are sitting on the floor. One holds a remote-control car, the other a stuffed dinosaur that I vaguely recognize as being similar to one of Kayla's toys.

And I see the water trails running toward them.

I used to think I was precognitive, as I see things play out before they do. And right now, I know what's going to happen. The water is moving slowly, but it'll reach the children. They'll cry and scream, because that's what children do, right, when they're upset?

Hell, no, I'm not having that happen today as well.

"Excuse me," I call out. The woman doesn't turn around, so I try again, louder.

Still nothing.

One of the children twists his head and makes eye contact with me. His gaze is suspicious as he evaluates me.

"Could you get your mum for me?" I ask, trying to smile sweetly—Dylan says I have a severe kind of smile and that I've spooked Kayla on more than one occasion—and point at the woman. Then I wonder if that was a mistake, assuming she's his mother. What if she isn't? I shouldn't have assumed.

Thankfully, at that moment, the woman turns. She gives me a confused look. I'm half standing in my seat.

"Hi," I say. "I just wanted to say, I've spilled some water, and it's running down the bus, and I don't want the children to get wet. It's all over the floor."

"What?" She squints at me, then removes an earphone. "Gosh, it is stuffy in here."

She reaches up with one long arm and opens the window. A torrent of icy air blows directly into my face. My eyebrows feel like they're freezing rapidly.

I repeat what I said, but for some reason decide to elaborate and give more info—only I end up lying and I tell her it's my water bottle that's leaked. I mean, I don't want to get into explanations about washing machines.

"*My* water bottle has leaked?" The woman gives me a strange look and then peers down at the floor. "No, it's fine. And my bag's not wet."

"No, *my* water bottle," I say, louder. The engine of the bus seems to get louder too. More cold air whistles in through the window. Too much noise. Too much roaring. And it's bloody freezing now. "It has soaked the floor here, and I don't want the children getting soaked too as I think it's running down the bus."

She gives me a strange look, like she's humoring me. "Right." But she doesn't make a move to pick up either child.

Well, I tried. I—

"Water, mummy!" One of the children points, excitement in his voice.

She looks around, behind her, at the floor. At the *freaking lake* that's billowing from my bag. She picks up the first child. Her eyes are on me. "Oh dear. Have you had an accident?" Her voice is stern, and that look she's giving me… Oh God.

"What? No!" I feel heat rising to my face. Great. Now I look embarrassed—a sure way to make me appear guilty of having had *an accident*. "I'm just trying to help."

She swipes up the second child and—

The driver slams on the brakes, the bus lurches, skids a bit, and all the water sloshes forward. The sea of my washing machine disaster rushes under the feet of the second child, whom the woman's still holding in mid-air. Water slams against the front of the bus, by the driver's cabin.

I look up. A red light. Traffic lights. Right. I'm almost at my stop. Good. Thank God for that.

The driver doesn't say anything about the state of the bus floor when I get off, and I'm too embarrassed to bring it up.

Well, the bag is slightly lighter to carry now. Got to look on the bright side.

At exactly two minutes before my shift starts, I arrive at the center and I'm pretty sure my fingers have frozen into formation around the laundry bag's handles.

The center is a building on the outskirts of Exeter that the charity rents during the evenings, and ever since I realized I was asexual at uni, I've volunteered here. Mrs. Mitchell owns the charity, and it's all about helping others cope with being ace or talk through feelings around asexuality. She used to be my teacher, then she was an actor, then she ran dating holidays for aces, but ever since there was an ace hate crime in the area— two women were attacked by a man who said he could 'cure' them—she started the Places for Aces charity and the helpline.

I've volunteered here for just over a year, and in the last two months, I've been promoted to managing the helpline. I like my work here more than I ever thought I would. By day, I'm an interior designer, but at night, well for two-to-four nights a week, I'm a listener. I'm a voice at the end of the phone. And I help people.

Anyone who's ace or questioning can call us, just as we get calls from families and friends of aces. We provide a talking and listening service. Nothing too deep—if calls start to get into problematic territory, we have things we can say to steer the conversation back to things we're qualified to talk about. If any of the volunteers take problematic calls, they report to me, and if it's serious, I report it to Mrs. Mitchell and she sorts it out.

I rush into the little community kitchen. Thankfully, the washing machine isn't in use—I mean, who else brings their washing to work? I set about thawing my fingers enough to release my grip on the bag, and then shove the load in. I add the gel that I tossed into my bag at the last moment in my kitchen, and I start the machine, before racing into the main room where the telephone sets are. Mrs. Mitchell is in today and is already on a call. She waves at me, as does Peter, a guy in his sixties who also volunteers here. He's not at his desk, but over by the counter, flicking through a ring-binder.

"Ah," he says, lifting one finger and pointing at something on a page. "Right. Got it."

I've no idea what he's got from the ring-binder, but he takes a page out of it, meanders back to his desk, and picks up his phone and dials. "Hello, yes, it's Christian from Places for Aces, returning your call. I've got that phone number that you wanted now."

We each have what Mrs. Mitchell calls a 'code name' for our work here, though Mrs. Mitchell uses her own name. But she insisted us volunteers use pseudonyms to protect us, just in case we get people phoning up who hate us or something, like that man who carried out the hate crimes.

The phone on my desk rings the moment I sit down. For the split second before I answer it, I try to guess who the caller will be. Someone new to the ace spectrum and trying to work out where they are on it? The annoyed partner of an ace who doesn't believe asexuality is a thing? The concerned parent who's overly worried that they'll never get grandchildren after their child has just come out as ace? Because, let's face it, at the moment we get more calls from people worrying about or being annoyed about someone being ace than actual calls from ace people themselves.

"Hello, you're through to the Places for Aces helpline. You're speaking to Tabitha." My voice is light and airy. "How can I help you?"

"Hello," a woman's voice says. "So, I... Well I don't know why I'm phoning really. I just found this leaflet from your organization, and I felt like I had to phone."

"That's okay," I say, praying that the woman isn't someone who'll then spout a spiel about how unnatural ace people are. She sounds posh, upper class. The kind of person who either went to St. Bridget's or who sends their children there. Although when I was there, I was on a scholarship and didn't have an upper-class accent at that time, Dylan has assured me I've since developed one. And I suppose he's right. I am careful of the way I speak now. Especially on the helpline—because people are way more argumentative with me on the days when

I'm not as careful to hide my Devon Farmer accent, especially if they've picked up the phone with a bone to pick. If this caller does show prejudice, it wouldn't be the first time it's happened.

You're unnatural. We evolved to want sex. You go against Gods work.

"Just take your time," I say. "If there's anything you'd like to ask, just let me know. Or we can chat about anything really."

That is what Mrs. Mitchell put in the script. It's supposed to make the caller feel at ease, that this is a safe space. But it often makes me uncomfortable, because so many people see it as a way to launch into topics that I'm no way qualified to deal with. And sure, sometimes asexuality can occur alongside trauma and abuse, but I'm not a therapist.

"What's your name?" I ask.

"Sophie." She clears her throat. "I guess the thing is, I don't know if I'm asexual." She breathes out hard. "Hell, I hadn't even expected it to be difficult just to say the word. But for so long, I thought I was broken. I knew I didn't feel like other people did... like my friends at school. We were at this boarding school, and it was all girls. And they were always talking about men. Well, boys. And I just... I never got it. Even though I said I did. I pretended because I didn't want to be different. When all the time, I just felt like I was an alien. I was different. It wasn't that I wasn't attracted to men, because I think I was. Well, I am. But not for sex. I want relationships, but just the thought of what happens in the bedroom, it makes my stomach curdle. And my ex, he said I needed to get therapy for this. He was sure I'd been abused and explained that that would be why I have this problem. But I wasn't abused. I'm sure of that. And yet... He's right. I'm broken. Or at least I thought I was until I saw your leaflet."

"Thank you for sharing that, Sophie. It must've been really difficult for you to open up about that, especially that treatment from a previous partner." I keep my tone smooth and soft, just as Mrs. Mitchell taught me. "But not wanting sex and not feeling sexual attraction are both valid things to feel." While I speak, I pull open my desk drawer where our leaflets are and take one out. On the cover, 'I'm not broken, I'm asexual' is written in bold letters.

"It *was* a relief," she says. "To know I wasn't the only one. I Googled it last night, after I saw the leaflet—it was just at this hotel, on the counter. I didn't expect to see anything like that there, and it was a relief—but I don't know. I feel weird. So weird. Like, for so long I thought I was broken, that something was wrong with me. And I'm relieved now to know this is a thing, but I still feel ashamed. Like, I just can't shake it."

"That's a perfectly normal thing to feel, and you're not alone. It's common for asexual people to be made to feel that way, because of the way we're brought up and the ideologies prevalent in society. But I want to reassure you that there's nothing to be ashamed of about being asexual."

"Thanks." She laughs. "And I mean, it makes me feel bad now, because... Oh lord. This isn't going to make me sound great."

"It's okay," I say. "This is a judgement-free zone."

There's a slight pause. "Well, I guess part of me wonders if I knew subconsciously I was asexual all along. Because when I was a teenager I was at this all-girls school, and one of our teachers was ace."

I lean forward. *I* was at an all-girls school, and a teacher there was ace. Ms. Trenway. I remember her now. She wasn't exactly liked by a lot of us. I mean, we thought she was a bit weird, and not just because she was asexual. It was more the way she dressed, but the aceness was something that many people equated with her weirdness. Didn't distinguish the weirdness from her sexuality—a lot of people thought one caused the other, that being ace *meant* she was weird.

"And she wasn't well-liked, this teacher," Sophie says. "And, uh, there were these rumors about her being plant-like or an alien."

I frown. *Wait.*

"And *I* was the one who started those rumors," Sophie says. "I made her life so difficult, and she took early retirement, and I think it was because of me. Because of what I did."

Wait. *Sophie.* My eyes widen. It's Sophie Sway. It has to be. There's no mistaking that posh voice. We went to the same boarding school.

And we absolutely hated each other.

TWO

Sophie

I WATCH MS. TRENWAY and feel revulsion curl through me. She's just so...weird. She looks like she should be in the Victorian era, what with her long skirts and dusty jackets. Her glasses are thick and rim-horned style, and she always checks the time on a pocket watch.

"Now, now! Class," she says, waving her hands about.

"Now, now, class," I mock, waving my own hands. The girls around me laugh, just as I knew they would. Janey and Rebecca and Stacey always laugh at whatever I do. They're my best friends and we're solid. A unit.

"Don't you think it's weird?" I ask, keeping my voice low. "Like there's something wrong with her?"

I still can't believe how Ms. Trenway just started talking about asexuality yesterday during the supervised homework hour. When Zoe, one of the other girls whom I don't really like, was making an inclusive LGBT+ poster with all the different flags on for citizenship work, Ms. Trenway had practically blown a gasket that she'd not drawn the asexual flag.

"I always knew she was weird," Rebecca says. "Ever since she told us she wasn't married. I mean, if she dressed in modern clothes she'd look okay. But, nah, she's not modern. I mean, what modern woman doesn't want sex?"

"Right," I say. "There's all this movement toward accepting women who like sex, and yet she's trying to undo it. Saying that she doesn't feel sexual attraction. I mean, that's obviously a lie." I laugh.

"Maybe she's just embarrassed about being a virgin," Stacey suggests. "Like she could be really frigid, and she's what, like eighty? And she doesn't want to admit it? I bet that's what this asexuality nonsense really is. Because it just doesn't make sense that it would exist. We're programmed to want sex, to breed, to reproduce. Yet she wants to pretend she's a robot."

"Will you be quiet?" Ms. Trenway bellows, her face red. Her beady eyes are fixed on our table. "Or perhaps you'd like to take over the teaching?" She hands a whiteboard pen toward me. "I'm sure, Ms. Sway, that you must be absolutely familiar with how to rearrange these equations, else why would you be talking about something other than mathematics?"

I feel my face redden a little. Did she hear us? I look at Stacey who's gone pale. Well, Stacey said the worst things anyway—not me. What I said wasn't even that bad. I didn't call her a robot or frigid.

Ms. Trenway shakes the pen at me. She's literally waiting for me to take the pen and take over.

Well, okay then.

I smile as brightly as I can and stand, taking the pen. I'm confident enough to walk to the board and make a mess of the equation because I know it'll just make the majority of the class laugh. The only ones who won't are the Davenports: Courtney and the twins, Zara and Zoe. They just hate me. Well, Courtney and I have had this huge rivalry going since Year Seven. We were both vying for first place in the St. Bridget's Got Talent Competition that they held in our first term at this school, and she won. Of course, I won the next year, but that didn't matter. It had started our rivalry—and that's never lessened.

When the twins joined in Year Nine, two years ago, they automatically took Courtney's side in everything. Really, it's a shame for them—they're pretty enough to have joined me and my friends, but apparently family loyalty meant they felt they couldn't leave Courtney. I'm just glad I haven't got any siblings or cousins. Just me and my dad. Though, of course, I do wish my mum was still with us.

The numbers on the whiteboard blur in front of me. Hell, some of them are those pesky letters—Ys and Xs—and it's all stupid anyway. I'm studying English at uni, once I've got my A-levels. Not going to need to know algebra beyond my GCSEs.

I doodle on the board, taking my time. Ms. Trenway breathes heavily behind me. I'm sure her nostrils will be flaring wide with each breath—that's one of the traits that gave her the nickname of 'the dragon.' Maybe that should be 'the virgin dragon' now. I disguise a laugh as a cough, and then I sign the board, next to my doodling, just for good measure.

"Well, Ms. Sway seems to think she's too popular to get detention," Ms. Trenway says, "but that is not the case. See me this afternoon after fifth period. Don't be late, else I'll be going to the headmaster about the topic of your conversation."

Courtney, at the table on the far side of the room, smiles. Zara and Zoe nudge each other, and then the three of them are whispering together.

I walk back to my table, a slight rushing sound in my ears. Hell, like I'll be attending detention tonight—it's Creative Writing Club with Mr. Rodgers. Ms. Trenway can't stop me from going to that. No, I'll phone Dad later, and he'll get it sorted. Our family donates too much to this school for them to treat me like this. Ms. Trenway needs to learn that.

The rest of the class passes rather undramatically. I keep my head down a bit more than I usually do, and I don't actually copy all my answers from Rebecca and Janey—no point copying Stacey as she always gets the answers wrong anyway. And I need to keep my grades up.

The bell rings, and I am already halfway out the room, my phone in my hand, ready to call Dad, when a figure blocks my way. Courtney Davenport. How the hell did she move so quickly?

"I heard what you and the posse were saying about Mrs. T." Her eyes are narrowed. "And that's not cool."

"What we were saying?" I snort. "You shouldn't have been eavesdropping."

"You shouldn't have been spouting all that acephobic stuff." She folds her arms. "It's the twenty-first century, for God's sake, Sophie. We're supposed to be inclusive of all sexualities."

"But asexual.*" I smirk. "Stacey's right anyway. That's just made up for people who are straight, who are just scared of sex or something."*

Courtney looks me up and down. "You've really got no idea. So, you shouldn't be spouting lies and nonsense about things you know nothing about. It's harmful."

Woah. What's got her knickers in a twist? Unless... My eyes widen. "Oh, so you think you're one of them too, these asexual aliens?" I laugh. I hear footsteps behind me, and I can tell it's Janey and Rebecca and Stacey—they've got a lot of perfume on, as always.

Courtney's eyes darken. "My sexuality is none of your business. And you want to be careful, Sophie. St. Bridget's doesn't tolerate hate talk like this."

I snort. "Oh, I'm really scared, Courbet."

Courtney's brow furrows—she hates that nickname, but of course that's why we use it. She looks me up and down, then she walks away, flicking her braids behind her shoulder. She wears two of them, always. I think the hairstyle looks childish. I mean doesn't she want to look her age? But Courtney doesn't wear make-up like the rest of us. She's always bare faced. Doesn't even cover up acne. It's like she wants to pretend the zits aren't there.

God, she's such a child. Huh. Maybe that's why she's scared of sex. Because that has to be why she's jumping on this asexual bandwagon. Either that or she likes Ms. Trenway. Huh.

"*Let's get to the canteen,*" Stacey says, "*before they sell out of the cheese toasties.*"

We move as a group, and as we get to the main corridor, the younger kids move aside for us. See, we're that powerful. Only I'm not really focusing on that. I'm turning over what Courtney was saying, over and over in my mind.

I lean toward Janey, Rebecca, and Stacey. "*Did you hear that? Courbet fancies Mrs. T!*"

Janey's eyes widen so much they look like they'll burst and spray eye-juice everywhere. "*Oh my God? Really?*"

"*It would make sense,*" Stacey says.

"*And I'm making the PowerPoint for tonight's assembly,*" I remind them. "*This should be fun.*"

Janey, Rebecca, and Stacey all insist we have front row seats at the assembly—even though it makes us stand out. I tried to stop them, but they insisted. We never normally sit this close to the front, and we've displaced some geeky-looking Year Sevens. But they moved quickly, no questions, after Janey glared at them.

"*And we have the details for this year's trip to Zambia to the orphanage,*" Mr. Webber says. He clicks the clicker in his hand, and the PowerPoint slide changes.

Already, I can feel the girls' excitement. Janey can barely sit still, Rebecca is breathing hard and fast, and Stacey keeps sending quick glances my way. I give them all a small smile. Just wait. The surprise is at the end.

It was so easy to add that extra slide in. Didn't take me long, just did it at the end of lunch, after I'd spoken to my dad—who assured me that he'd get my stupid detention with Ms. Trenway cancelled. I mean, who does that woman think she is?

For the third time since assembly started, I turn in my seat and look at Courtney. She's six rows behind us, but the girl's freakishly tall, and she's a whole head above everyone else.

On the stage, Mr. Webber drones on and on about what a perfect opportunity volunteering at the Zambian orphanage is, how it'll just make our UCAS applications shine and make universities desperate to have us.

Huh. As if I need help like that. I'm going to Oxford. My grades are good, and all my family went there. It's my birth right.

Janey shakes with so much excitement she looks like she's desperate for the loo, and her excitement gets more and more tangible as the PowerPoint progresses.

Then Mr. Webber clicks the clicker, and there's a large intake of breath from all around the assembly hall. And from me—this isn't the slide I added! This is...

"What the hell?" I turn and look at Janey—Janey who is grinning from ear to ear. Shit. I left her to save the PowerPoint as I had my clarinet lesson and the computer had frozen. And this—the photo on the slide— is of Ms. Trenway and Courtney from last year, when we had a school trip to a nature reserve. The two of them paired up for the challenges as our class had an odd number. I was with Janey, and Stacey and Rebecca went together. Poor Courtney having to go with Ms. Trenway.

"Wait for it," Janey says, giving me a grin.

My stomach churns. "What the hell have you done?"

But Janey just nods at the screen.

"What is this?" Mr. Webber splutters, frowning at the photo. He clicks the clicker again, and words appear on the screen.

NO WONDER THEY LOOK SO HAPPY. TWO ASEXUAL ALIENS TOGETHER.

THREE

Courtney

DYLAN AND KAYLA are sitting on a bench, each clutching huge ice creams despite the temperature, when I arrive the next morning. My head is pounding, and I didn't sleep well. All night, I tossed and turned, knowing I'd spoken to a caller whom I knew—and I didn't disclose it to her. I just continued the call, no matter how uneasy I was feeling. Just listened to her as she confided to me about being ace and how she feels broken, and she didn't know it was me. And now I know this hugely personal thing about Sophie Sway, and she doesn't even know I know. It makes me feel dishonest, and it's probably unethical.

"So, what are we planning for my birthday?" Dylan asks, then bites into his ice cream, leaving huge teeth marks. I just don't get how he can bite ice cream and not get brain freeze. Especially when there's still frost on the ground here. He and Kayla must be the only people in the world to eat ice cream in this weather.

"You mean, what am *I* planning?" I correct him, and I try to concentrate on that—on his birthday surprise, and not on Sophie Sway. "Well, it wouldn't be a surprise if I told you."

Dylan sighs and a trickle of ice cream drips down the cone. "Court, I don't like surprises."

"Trust me. You'll like this one," I say.

Kayla giggles and then licks her ice cream delicately. She's wearing her fluffy pink gloves and holds her cone so tightly, and every now and again, she adjusts her grip on the cone with a lot of concentration. Last time I met up with them like this, she dropped her cone and was so upset. I bought her an extra large one to make up for it. I hate it when she cries. She just looks so sad, and my heart aches when she's upset.

Dylan sighs again—a more dramatic sigh this time. "Well, I suppose it's just one day a year."

"Really, you'll like it. I guarantee it."

I glance at my phone. It's Monday, but I'm not working today, so I could start the planning later. I wonder if I can get the twins over to help me too? They'll both be working today, but maybe this evening will work. I fire off some quick texts. Planning a party is exactly what I need to distract me from Sophie and the looming guilt inside me that I've done something wrong.

Once Kayla and Dylan have finished their ice creams, we walk toward the pond at the end of the park to see the ducks. Kayla watches them with big eyes, and Dylan produces a bag of sweetcorn for her to throw to them. It's turning out to be a lovely day. Cold, yes, but the sky's becoming a really vivid blue. The air's clear.

"Ducky!" Kayla whispers, and it's always her quiet excitement that awes me.

We spend half an hour more at the park, before Dylan says it is time to go. He's teaching a meditation class later and needs to get Kayla to his mum's house. We say a quick goodbye—and Dylan reminds me again not to prepare anything too extravagant or embarrassing for his birthday..

When I get back to my block, a huge removals van is parked right outside my living room window. I love having a ground-floor flat. Even if this does happen a fair bit. It was kind of Mrs. Dalton to warn me of this, but it's not like it's a new thing. Whenever anyone in Hawklands gets food delivered, the supermarket vans park in the exact same spot too, casting the majority of my apartment into darkness.

I head through the communal corridor, searching with one hand for the keys in my bag. My fingers brush against my bottle of hand gel, my purse, my phone, and the tattered paperback I keep in there for emergencies before I locate my keys. I pull them out, but they snag on something. Frowning, I peer into my bag, still walking, and—

"Oh, I'm so sorry!" I say as I crash into someone.

"It's fine." But the woman has a voice that most definitely indicates it's *not* fine.

"I wasn't looking where I was going—I'm so sorry." My words tumble out too quickly. They always do when I'm flustered and—

I stare at the woman with blond hair. It's dead straight and sleek. Her lips have a touch of pink gloss on them, and her blue eyes are wide as she stares at me.

"Courtney?" she says.

Oh no. This can't be happening. It can't. It really can't.

She looks at me. It's her. Definitely her.

"What are you doing here?" she asks.

But before I can answer her, a high-pitched voice yells, "Fifi!"

I turn to see Mrs. Dalton torpedoing toward us, and I step back just in time to avoid being knocked over.

Fifi? This is Fifi? Oh hell no.

Talking to her on the helpline was bad enough.

There's no way I can *live* next to Sophie Sway.

"What are you doing here?" Sophie repeats.

I take an uncertain step back. "I live here."

"You two know each other?" Mrs. Dalton's face is very pink.

"We went to the same school," Sophie says, tight-lipped.

Mrs. Dalton clasps her hands together. "How wonderful! Oh, you must come in at once, Courtney. How lovely for Fifi to have a friendly face around here that isn't one of us oldies." She laughs.

A friendly face. I want to laugh. I'm not a friendly face to Sophie, just as she isn't to me.

"And just what are the chances of this happening?" Mrs. Dalton is gushing so much her face is now changing from pink to red—and it's very shiny too. Sweaty. Lovely. "What a small world it is. How lovely for you both. Did you stay in touch after school? Did you know you'd both be living here?"

"No, we didn't stay in touch," Sophie says, and she at least has the decency to look sheepish. Embarrassed.

Good. She deserves to feel uncomfortable. I fold my arms.

"Not to worry," Mrs. Dalton says. "You can go shopping together and to the cinema and whatever else it is millennials like to do."

"Actually," I say. "We weren't friends at school. At all."

"Ah, different friendship groups." Mrs. Dalton nods. "But this has to be fate! Courtney, we're all going for a meal tomorrow lunchtime to welcome Fifi, so you'll have to join us."

A meal? With them? I nearly freeze. "Sorry, I have plans."

"But you'll want to catch up with Fifi." She says it like a statement, not a question.

I glance at Sophie. She's looking anywhere but at me.

"Actually," I say. "I don't have very favorable memories of Sophie. We weren't friends."

Mrs. Dalton's mouth drops into an O shape, and she stares at me then at Sophie.

"We didn't like each other," Sophie says at last.

"My goodness," Mrs. Dalton says, turning to Sophie. "Is this the girl you had that...trouble with? You know, your father told me about those things that happened at school, the accusations that were made against you."

Sophie's face reddens. "Look, we're all adults now. We can move on. And anyway"—she glances at me—"it's not like Courtney and I are going to be bosom buddies now."

I nod a little, and Sophie nods back. Mrs. Dalton is still doing her fish impression.

"I'd best be off," I say, indicating the door to my flat. It's only a few feet away.

Before either of them can say anything more, I retreat and lock myself securely in my apartment. My heart pounds ten to the dozen, and I drop my bag onto the floor, clenching my keys to my chest.

This *cannot* be happening.

"I cannot live next door to her!" I tell my mum, gripping my phone hard.

"She could've matured a lot since then," Mum says. "People change. They grow up."

"No, I don't want to live next door to her. When I graduated from St. Bridget's, I thought I'd never have to see her again—only now I'm going to have to. It's just…" Tears pinch the corners of my eyes, and oh my God, Sophie's making me cry—still.

I take several deep breaths and then start pacing the apartment.

"Well, just calm down," Mum says. "Look, didn't your neighbor say she's only staying for a little while?"

"*A little while* is still too long. She made my life hell! And you know what she was like to Zara and Zoe."

Mum makes a noise deep in her throat—it's her thinking noise. "Well, then you have to make her want to move out sooner."

"But how can I do that?" I whisper. My heart is still pounding. I head into my bedroom and pace around there, to the big bay window—where I find my missing snow boots, complete with Sergeant Ginger Paws asleep in one of them.

"Use your initiative," Mum says. "But, darling, I'm sorry, I have to go now. My appointment's in five minutes."

"It's okay, thanks." I nudge the boot with the sleeping cat, but he doesn't stir. Just continues snoring—he's actually snoring. That's kind of delightful.

"Talk at the weekend okay?" Mum says.

"Sure, yes. Thanks."

I end the call only feeling slightly better. But Mum's right—there must be something I can do to make Sophie *want* to leave sooner. I scrunch my nose as I think—and then the answer just sails toward me.

Sophie is scared of ghosts.

I smile. I know exactly what to do. Then she'll move away, and she'll never find out that I'm also Tabitha from the helpline. And I'll never have to see her again.

But first—step one of my rapidly forming plan. I pull out my phone and Google 'how to make someone think their house is haunted.'

FOUR

Sophie

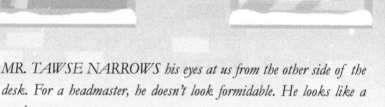

MR. TAWSE NARROWS his eyes at us from the other side of the desk. For a headmaster, he doesn't look formidable. He looks like a weed.

"This is not acceptable, girls," he says. "You cannot imply that a teacher and a student are in a relationship when it's a baseless accusation that nonetheless has real-world implications. And you cannot out another student like that."

"Who said anything about outing?" Janey snorts. She's sitting right next to me, and Rebecca and Stacey are on Janey's other side. "I wasn't doing that."

"If indeed Courtney Davenport is asexual, then you have just outed her to the whole school, all for a bit of entertainment, and you've also been very derogatory. What was it you called her and Ms. Trenway? Aliens? That's hate speech, girls, and we do not tolerate that here."

"Well, I'm sorry." Janey sniffs. She doesn't look sorry though, and part of me wants to kill her. She was way out of line with that—and I saw the look of hurt on Courtney's face as we were all filing out.

I'd tried to speak to her, tried to tell her it was all Janey—but Courtney just barked at me to get out of her way. And I did. I watched as she fled, and I've never hated Janey, my supposed best friend, so much.

"Sorry isn't good enough." Mr. Tawse has food in his moustache, and I focus on that as he speaks. "The damage has been done, and I have no choice now but to discuss your behavior with the governors to see if St Bridget's can continue offering a place for each of you."

I snort, then I realize he's serious. "Are you for real? Look, Janey was the one did this. Not us." I glance at her, but honestly, she deserves being thrown under the bus. Courtney and I may have a rivalry going—one that's been in place since our early days here as eleven-year-olds—but it's never been bullying. And that's what this is.

"But you were the one who was responsible for the PowerPoint, in the first place, Sophie. And you should've worked on it alone—not got your friends to do it. And I find it hard to believe that you didn't know what the contents of that slide was."

"But I didn't—look, it was supposed to be a funny meme, that's all." I shoot a look at Janey, before turning back to Mr. Tawse. "And you can't kick me out. My father pays for half this school. He'll withdraw all his donations if you kick me out."

"You cannot threaten me," he says. "And the fact of the matter is we owe Courtney a duty of care, and we need to make this place a good place for her. You've undone that, and it may be that we cannot keep you here, for it could very well be detrimental to her mental health."

"You can't kick us out though," Stacey says, speaking for the first time. She looks at Rebecca, who nods.

Janey leans forward. "Look, if Courbet—I mean, Courtney." She laughs. "If she's too traumatized or whatever now, then just suggest that she moves schools. She's a scholarship student anyway. You wouldn't be losing anything."

Mr. Tawse purses his lips. "I don't think you're understanding the gravity of this situation, and I cannot be blackmailed on this. I will be talking to the governors, about you. In the meantime, you will all be attending Isolation for all lessons."

"Isolation?" I narrow my eyes at him. How am I supposed to maintain good grades if I'm not even being taught by the right teachers? Isolation just has a cover-teacher in there all the time. And I need to keep my grades high if I want to get into Oxford. "Just wait until my father hears about this."

Mr. Tawse stands. It just makes him look even more weedy. "Money does not give you the right to bully others. Now, report to Isolation tomorrow. If you don't, there will be repercussions."

And, with that, the bell rings, signifying the end of the day. Well, at least we missed the last lesson.

"Off you go."

I go—while firing a quick text to my father. He'll sort out this nonsense.

The next day, it's Miss Aylott manning Isolation . She used to be one of my favorite teachers—until the day she delivered the bad news. Now, whenever I see her, I can't help but be reminded of that day.

Miss Aylott admits us into isolation one-by-one. I'm first, and she indicates one of the free booths for me to sit in. It already has my name written on a folded piece of paper.

The Isolation Centre is a large room at the top of campus, and it houses eight individual booths. Each booth has a desk, a laptop, and a chair. There's a bottle of water on each desk, along with a clear pencil case containing two pens, two pencils, a sharpener, and an eraser.

I sit down slowly. There's one other person already in Isolation today, but she looks about twelve so I doubt she's going to spread any shit about me or my friends being here. And if she does, she'll soon learn not to.

"Your phone please," Miss Aylott says.

I turn to see her outstretched hand behind me. Reluctantly, I place my phone in her palm. My dad still hasn't replied to my texts. Guess I'll have to wait until later.

"The laptop is already loaded with your work," Miss Aylott says. "But if you've any questions, let me know."

I nod and settle down, and she goes out for the next girl. I don't know why we have to be brought in one at a time, and I bet Janey's been talking some more shit about me out there to Rebecca and Stacey, after I told Mr. Tawse it was all her. She was doing that all evening yesterday. It was pathetic. And when we walked over here from Breakfast, she'd glowered at me—but really, what does she expect? She went way too far.

Stacey's next to be admitted into Isolation, and she's directed to the booth next to me. Her eyes are wide and buggy, and her nostrils quiver as she walks past me. Once she's in the booth, I can't see her thanks to the partition walls that separate the booths, but I can hear her shaky breaths, how she's trying not to cry.

A few minutes later, Janey's inside. "Bitch," she hisses at me, and I don't know how Miss Aylott doesn't hear her.

Once Rebecca's inside too, I try to concentrate on my work—even if the laptop here is slow. And the WiFi's so patchy. But I suppose it is quite nice being in Isolation. It's peaceful. Miss Aylott returns to her desk at the front, her heels clip-clopping. A quick flick of my head tells me she's busy doing marking or whatever it is on her desk, so she's not even hovering over us like a hawk.

I get a surprising amount of work done before Miss Aylott tells me and the others it's break time. Guess we're too far away from the main buildings to hear the bell here. The Year Seven is up and out like a shot, as are Janey, Stacey, and Rebecca, but I take my time as I move toward Miss Aylott. She's still at her desk.

"Can I have my phone?" I ask her. I need to send another message to Courtney or something. She didn't reply to my messages yesterday evening, and I couldn't find her when I searched. I need to make sure she's okay.

Miss Aylott holds my gaze for a moment. Then she says, "Sophie," and her voice is soft and all melodic. "How are you doing?"

"How am I doing?" I stare at her in surprise.

"I understand how difficult things have been for you since your mother passed away," she says, her voice simpering. "And I understand that sometimes grief manifests in strange ways. You're hurting, so you want to make others hurt."

"This has nothing to do with my mother's death," I snap, feel heat rush to my face. I don't want to talk about that. I've been doing just fine without talking about it.

"Only we have noticed the timing," Miss Aylott says. "I know that as soon as you and Courtney both joined in Year Seven, you saw each other as rivals. It was amicable though, apart from the odd, unkind word. But since your mother's passing, many of us have noticed how much you've suddenly turned on Courtney. Not just you, but your friends too. It is clearly a reaction."

"It's not a reaction," I say, only I can't then help thinking about how much I dislike Perfect Courtney. And maybe what Miss Aylott is saying has some truth to it. Because right after I heard that my mother had been killed in a car accident, I saw Courtney with her mum. It was the parents' day at our school, at the end of last year, and my mother and father were supposed to be here. Their car had been hit an hour before they were due to arrive. My mother was pronounced dead at the scene, my father taken to the hospital. He sent word to the school.

Then, Miss Aylott pulled me to the side and gently explained what had happened and said she'd drive me to the hospital to see my father. Just as we were leaving, we passed Courtney and her mother. Her mother who was wrapping her arms around her, who looked so pretty and motherly. Courtney still had her mother and I didn't. It wasn't fair.

But still—I didn't want this to happen to Courtney. And sure, I've upped my game a bit with the rivalry, but it's been harmless. Until now.

"My phone?" I glare at Miss Aylott.

She hands it to me. "Don't be late back."

FIVE

Sophie

I LOOK AROUND the bedroom—Victoria Dalton, my step mother, said it was mine, especially for me, but it's clearly the guest room. Pale blue quilt on the bed, navy blue curtains, and a turquoise carpet. Still, I suppose it is nice of her to offer me a place while I sort myself out. Even if she feels obliged to do so. She'd only been married to my father for three years before he died. I expected her to faze me out of her life completely—only she didn't. She called constantly to see how I was, invited me on days out with her and her son, and told me that I'd always be a part of the family.

And now I'm living with her—and Victoria seems *happy* about it. I shake my head. I still can't quite believe it.

"I think this is the last box," Victoria says as she staggers into the room with a box marked 'books.' She looks relieved when she's put it on the desk. I suppose that box is rather heavy.

"Thank you," I say. "Is the front door locked?"

"Locked?" She frowns. "Not yet."

My heart beats a little faster. "But you'll lock it, won't you?"

"Of course—but you don't need to be worried. People are lovely around here."

Worried—well, that seems to be all I am now. Worried that *he* is going to come after me.

Victoria moves to the window and straightens the curtain. "You know, I think you should apologize to Courtney."

"I already did—at the time."

"I mean now," she says.

I roll my eyes, and she tuts at me.

"It wouldn't hurt to make an effort, given she's our neighbor. And she's looked after my animals many a time— especially when Sergeant keeps getting in her place. Plus, Arthur did too, once. Don't know how, but there he was, flying around her kitchen. Fifi, I don't want things to be awkward. So, you'd better make peace with her."

"I will." I shrug. Like Courtney's going to want to listen to anything I've got to say though. "What does she do?"

"Do?"

"For a living."

"Ah, she's an interior designer at a firm in Exeter. God, I can't remember the name of it now—that's what menopause does to you. So many hot flushes, and my memory's never been so bad." She laughs, but her laugh is too high-pitched. She's nervous.

I try not to look too happy about the fact Courtney works at a firm because that means she's not her own boss. And I am—or at least I will be. And I'm clearly winning between the two of us yet again.

I don't know why I always have this need to be competitive. It's not just around Courtney it surfaces, but it's pretty much there with every woman I encounter. It's why I realized I had to be my own boss in the end, setting up Sophie Says Shop—which will go live next month. It's a virtual personal shopping experience. I've got some big-name brands on board now, and they give me and my clients a 5% discount. The smaller brands give a 10% discount. So of course wannabes fashionistas choose me to shop for them. I'm Sophie Sway, as seen on TV, dressing models, and they can also get brand name clothes cheaper with me. Win win. And then the money from that will fund my real loves: writing and acting.

Just a shame I lost the London flat. Anger flares up as I think of what happened. Of Adam and how he gambled the flat away, leaving me homeless. I don't know what he's doing or where he is now, but I don't care so long as he stays away from me.

"I'll go and get a takeaway," Victoria says. "You still like Hawaiian pizza?"

"Of course," I say, but my stomach's already tying itself in knots at the thought of greasy food. "Thanks."

That evening, after I've eaten two small slices of pizza and tried not to panic about the calories, and then watched a film with Victoria and her son—I still can't think of Martin as my step-brother—I'm exhausted by the time I get into bed. But, despite the exhaustion, I can't fall asleep quickly. I never can now—I imagine things. Footsteps. Doors opening.

And I know the front door is locked because I checked it three times, and my window in this room isn't open, so I know I'm safe. But I just don't feel like I am.

I pull out my phone and earphones from the bedside cabinet's drawer and—

Shit. There's another message. From him.

Adam.

His face swims into my mind, unbidden. Angular jaw, blond hair, sunburnt skin, and eyes that pierce you. My hands seize up, holding onto my phone so tightly, like it's suddenly got a hundred times heavier. I flinch as I recall the last words he said to me—how he said I was an ungrateful bitch because his 'efforts' at making a living weren't good enough, when in reality all he did was gamble away everything he could get his hands on.

I don't want to look at his text—anything that he has to say now can't be good. He isn't one to back down, and he'll never realize just how much he hurt me. But I steel myself and open the text—it's better to know than not.

You can't just leave me. I'm going to find you.

I read his text in his voice. Croaky, a smoker's cough. Emphasis on the last word in each sentence.

Coldness fills my heart, spreads out across my chest, my back. I swallow hard and then scroll back up the message stream. It's been three weeks since I replied to him, three weeks since he gambled our flat away, right before Christmas, three weeks of him sending me messages like this.

But he's not going to find me. Not here—we're far enough away from London here, in South Devon. That's why I eventually asked Victoria if I could stay with her while I sorted myself out. Because her apartment is farther away than any of my friends, who are all in London. Every night I slept on their sofas, hopping from one to another for a week or so, I knew I was still too close to Adam.

I never want to see him again.

Trying to clear my head, I put on the meditation app. Victoria suggested I got it a few years back. She goes to a weekly meditation group in town run by some hippie guy—no doubt she'll be dragging me along too, now I'm living here and 'unemployed' as she called it. Victoria simply doesn't get that I'm not unemployed. I'm *self*-employed—even if my business hasn't officially launched.

"Maintain your breathing," the low, gentle voice of the app says. "Concentrate on breathing in for…" I lose my concentration on the app and the meditation and breathing because I can hear something.

Footsteps?

I take one earphone out and listen. *Yes.* There it is. But it's not footsteps. Something is making a tapping sound. But then it stops.

I frown and listen. Everything's silent for a moment.

Until it happens again.

Tap. Tap. Tap.

Whatever it is, it's not Adam, I tell myself. It's not. I'm safe here. Safe with Victoria and Martin. But still I get out of bed and check the front door. Yes, still locked.

Back in my room, I put my earphones back in and try to ignore the tapping—maybe it's the water pipes or something. Yes, that'll be it.

I follow the app's instructions for ten minutes, and—

Tap. Tap. Tap.

I can't concentrate because of the tapping.

Oh my God. Irritation is turning to anger fast. I get out of bed and look carefully for the source of the tapping. Is it in here? What's going on? But I can't see anything that would account for it.

Tap. Tap. Tap.

I push open the door and step into the hall. The tapping is still continuing—but it's quieter out there—loudest in my room.

"You all right, dear?" Victoria calls from her room.

"Yes," I say.

I head back into my room. Maybe I'm imagining it.

Tap. Tap. Tap.

I grab the pillow and clamp it over head so it covers my ears. This is going to be a long night.

SIX
Courtney

AT WORK THE next day, Sally looks me up and down with a critical eye. She's nearing fifty, and the two of us are the only women in the office. We're also best friends, and everyone assumes it's girl solidarity and all that, and if there were other women my age here then I'd not be as good friends with Sally. But that's not true.

Sally may be almost twice my age, but we get on. She's fun and cool and sophisticated and I tell her about my little game with Sophie last night.

"Really, you did that in Morse code?" Sally snorts and pushes her glasses farther up her nose. She has awesome glasses—they're multi-colored and match her multi-colored hair.

I nod. *"The ghost of Amanda Bellamy welcomes you to the Hawklands."* I can't help but let out a short laugh. It'd taken me a moment to recall the layout of their flat—Mrs. Dalton invited me in one time, after returning Sergeant Ginger Paws. I'm pretty sure that their guest room is directly above my own bedroom. "Took me ages to work out the Morse code though.

And it's a good job I'm tall and could reach the ceiling, else I'd have had to use the broom handle."

"And this woman knows Morse code?" Sally gathers some papers from her desk and shoves them into her bag. It's lunch time and the two of us are heading out to a café. Sally always takes her work with her though. It's not that she'll be working on it when we're out, but rather that she doesn't trust graduate—the new recruit—not to take her work. Sally's very protective of her designs.

"She did at school." I nod vigorously. Sophie's clever, one of the cleverest people out there. "She was obsessed with brain training and keeping up her cognitive levels at school. I doubt she'll have let that slip. She did an interview a few years ago, after she won some modelling contest, where she was proving she wasn't a… oh, what was it? The wording… Not a Blonde Bimbo, or something." I roll my eyes. "Stereotypes or what?"

"Well, you'll have to let me know if it worked, this ghost stuff," Sally says as I grab my handbag. "And who's Amanda Bellamy?"

"No idea. But I thought the ghost needed to have a name to be believable."

Sally laughs.

We head out the office and take the elevator down two floors. Outside, it's still bitterly cold, and I'm glad for my thick coat. We hurry down the street and around the corner to where Little Bee's Café is. It's one of my favorite places to eat at—not just because the food's good and they can cater really well to allergies and dietary requirements, but because the staff there are so nice and they regularly donate a percentage of their profits to charity. Sally and I eat here every Tuesday, and we sit at our usual table in the far corner. The tablecloths have also got the cutest bees printed on them, and they match the tattoo I have on the back of my neck.

The waitresses and chef know us by name by now, and we exchange a few pleasantries before ordering. I go for my usual—Jacket potato with coronation chicken and salad— while Sally orders soup of the day.

"They do the best homemade bread I've ever tasted," she says, just as she says it every time we're here. "It's such a shame they don't make a gluten-free version of this, else I'd bring my son here."

I nod. My usual answer rolls smoothly off my tongue. "But their jacket potatoes are divine. They're absolutely huge."

We share a small laugh, before the waitress—Annie— delivers our drinks. Two cappuccinos.

"Thank you," Sally says to her, before leaning toward me. "So, Courtney, has anyone spoken to you about the library yet?"

I shake my head.

"Hmm." She frowns into her cappuccino. "I did specifically ask for *you* to be added. Asked him yesterday."

"Maybe John will do that later today then," I suggest.

She runs her hands through her hair. "We're working with JVK again." JVK Architecture and Designs are one of the big specialist architecture firms in Devon and Cornwall. We're only an hour's drive from their main office in Rose Haven. "And I was really hoping Jenna Lake would be assigned to this one," Sally says. "You know, she's that young one—by which I mean late twenties. Older than you." She laughs. "But Jenna's really nice. But no, we've got Malcolm—the doddery old one.

I'm telling you now, Courtney, he needs to retire. He's making mistakes—mistakes I've spotted, and I'm not even an architect. And then he has the audacity to say *my* designs are too outdated, and he doesn't want to work with a granny."

I raise my eyebrows. "Seriously? He said that? Isn't that ageism?"

Sally nods. "Yep. So, John said he'd add a 'young-un' to the library project too. I was hoping it would be you rather than Malcolm." She takes a large sip of her cappuccino. "I mean, how is he a 'young-un'? He's older than me!"

"We don't know it is Malcolm," I point out. "Still time for John to ask me and—"

"Oh my God," a voice says from behind me.

I turn, a cold sweat breaking out across my whole body. Sophie Sway is right behind me, standing in the doorway. Her eyes are frozen on me.

"Are you following me?" She stares at me.

"Uh, no. I was here first." I shoot a what-the-hell look at Sally.

"But this—this is where we're eating today. For the meal," Sophie says. "And Victoria's going to insist you join us if you're here. You and your…mum?" She glances at Sally, frowning a little.

"Oh, she's not…" I start to say, but I trail off as Mrs. Dalton steps into the building too, along with her son Martin.

Of course she sees me. Mrs. Dalton must have x-ray vision or something. She just knows if anyone is present whom she knows, and she knows it within like a fraction of a second.

"Courtney!" she sings. "Oh, how wonderful. You and your…friend…must join us. It will give us a chance to settle things between you and Fifi."

"It's *Sophie*," Sophie mutters. "And I really don't think Courtney wants to."

"Nonsense," Mrs. Dalton says. "Look, you two were just kids before. Kids are mean, and all that. But we're all adults now, and we can sort this. Who knows, the two of you may even be friends."

I let out a snort before I can stop myself.

"Is this her?" Sally stage-whispers to me, and Sophie's gaze snaps to her.

I nod.

"Of course we'll join you," Sally says before I can say anything. I widen my eyes at her, and Sally leans in close to me as she stands, gathering her bag and picking up her cappuccino. The mug clinks against the saucer. "You need to know your enemy, right?" she says in a low voice. "Then you can really excel at the ghost game."

"Right," I mutter, but then we're all moving tables and chairs—I throw a quick apologetic look to the waitresses who are looking flustered.

I end up seated between Mrs. Dalton and Sally. Sophie is directly opposite me, with Martin on her right, opposite Sally.

"Well, isn't this lovely?" Mrs. Dalton says.

"Lovely," we all say in varying tones of sincerity. Sophie looks so furious it almost makes it worth it, being seated with her.

A waitress takes the Dalton family's orders and asks Sally and I if we want our food when it's ready or at the same time as the rest of our party.

"As soon as it's ready, please," Sally says. "We've got a short lunch break, you see."

"So, what is it you do?" Mrs. Dalton asks Sally, and then the two of them launch into a very detailed conversation about what exactly it is that interior designers do and don't do.

Sophie, Martin, and I stare uncomfortably at each other for a good five minutes before Martin clears his throat.

"So, you're Courtney, right?" he asks me. He's looks about fifteen but I'm guessing he's older else he'd be in school.

"Yes," I say. He knows this. We've done the whole introductions thing at least six times since they moved in upstairs.

He looks at Sophie "And she's the same Courtney that you went to school with?".

"Yes," Sophie and I both say. Her tone is harsher than mine, and it's almost like my 'yes' shrinks into the background to get away from hers.

"Small world." Martin exhales hard.

I busy myself with drinking my cappuccino and praying for this all to be over soon. It's so awkward sitting here, opposite Sophie. My nemesis, my rival.

"You know, we really need to find a way for you two to get over your history and get on now," Mrs. Dalton says.

No, I think. *We don't have to do that at all.*

"How long is she staying?" I ask.

"I am right here," Sophie grumbles. She pushes back her blond hair, revealing her slender neck—and I suppose she does have a good figure. Not that I can see much when she's sitting down, but she's sitting bolt upright. Good posture, my mum would say. And Sophie's face is rather symmetrical. I can see why she was a model.

"Sorry." I feel my face flush with heat. "How long are you staying?"

"Just until I'm sorted," she says. "Then you'll never see me again."

Good. But I don't say the word—I just nod.

Mine and Sally's food arrives and although eating it with Sophie, Martin, and Mrs. Dalton watching me is incredibly awkward, it gives me an excuse not to say anything else.

The Daltons' food is only five minutes later than ours. Somehow Sophie manages to look dainty while eating her chicken salad. If that was me, I'd have ended up with the mayonnaise all over my face. As it is, I find myself taking smaller more delicate bites of my coronation chicken and potato, and cutting it up more neatly so I don't end up with food around my mouth—or worse, down my top.

Somehow, the Dalton family manages to finish at the same time as Sally and me, so we all end up leaving the café together, and there's an awkward moment where Mrs. Dalton hugs me and then Sally—Mrs. Dalton is definitely a hugger—and I'm left nodding at Sophie and Martin.

"Well, thank God I didn't have to hug Sophie too," I say to Sally as we leave.

Sally snorts. "You know, that wasn't half tense, was it? Could've cut the tension between the two of you with a knife. Must make it harder to hate her when you're attracted to her."

I freeze. "What?"

Sally gives me an odd look. "You barely took your eyes off her the whole time, Courtney. And you were mirroring her posture the whole time."

"I was not!"

"You were," she says. "And once more, she was watching you just as closely. I think there's something there."

Heat floods me.

No. Sally's wrong. I'm definitely not attracted to Sophie. Definitely not.

SEVEN

Sophie

"HEY." I NOD at Courtney, finally having cornered her. It's late in the evening now, and two days have passed since Janey went way too far.

Courtney's in the home room, her books spread around her, pen in hand. I slide into the chair on the opposite side of her table. My chest rises and falls too quickly. I'm nervous—but I've also spent ages running around school, trying to find Courtney.

Her eyes narrow as she looks at me. "What do you want?"

"Look, I'm so sorry—honestly, I am. I didn't know Janey had done that."

"Sure you didn't," Courtney mutters.

"Court, I wouldn't do that to you—look, we've always been cool. Yeah, we're rivals and that because we're the smartest people here, but I've never done anything to hurt you. Not like that. It was all Janey. I swear... I swear on the memory of my mother. You have to believe me."

Courtney's eyes soften a little. "Okay."

"Okay?" I lean back, surprised.

"Look, it doesn't really make a difference, either way," she says. "It's still been done. And people are still talking shit about me, and Ms. Trenway's still under investigation or something. So yeah, you're just doing this apology for yourself—so you can go now."

"F-f-for myself?" I splutter, looking at her. "No, I wanted to know that you're okay."

Courtney snorts. "Really? Sophie, we're not friends. You don't care about how I feel."

"But I do—look, I'm sorry that this has all happened. You and I..." I gesture at the space between us on the tabletop. "The rivalry was only supposed to be a game, that's all. You know, like at the spelling bee."

"Of course I know. I was there."

"I suppose Janey didn't understand the rules of our rivalry—she didn't realize that there's this mutual level of respect between us," I say, wondering if there is in fact still a mutual level of respect. "She took it too far, and what she did was awful."

"So, what are you going to do about it?" Courtney asks.

"Do?"

"About Janey," she says. "If you're saying this is all her, then what are you going to do?"

I breathe deeply. "I'll... I'll sort it, okay?"

Courtney nods, but her shoulders are still up by her ears—she's so tense now. "I will sort it, I promise."

"Really? We ignore Janey?" Stacey looks at me, one eyebrow raised.

I managed to catch her in the common room, just before curfew. We've only got a few minutes until the bell goes, and I think Janey's already in our room. I room with Janey, and Rebecca and Stacey room together.

"Yeah, and you'll tell Rebecca too? We've all got to do this."

Stacey smooths down her hair, then takes a band from her wrist and ties it into a messy bun which kind of makes the smoothing-down actions seem pointless. "Okay."

The two of us are silent, just looking at each other, until the bell rings, loud and clear. We move out into the corridor and toward the dorms. Only a few other students are about, and we get to the dorms in good time—before the second bell goes off.

Stacey disappears into room eighteen, and I open number twenty. The door creaks, and then clicks softly shut behind me. Janey's sprawled out on her bed, earphones in. Her music's so loud that I can hear the bass.

I sigh, rolling my eyes.

"All right, Soph?" Janey asks, taking one earphone out. She stopped glaring at me this morning. Seems to want things back to how they were.

I pull off my hoody and pointedly don't look in her direction as I arrange the garment on the back of my chair by my desk.

"Sophie?"

I hear Janey's bed creak, and out of the corner of my eye, I can see she's sitting upright now.

"Earth to Sophie?"

I hum under my breath as I check my phone. It's been on charge by my desk for a good few hours. A missed call from my father. He wasn't happy when I spoke to him before. Mr. Tawse had phoned him, told him that what happened in assembly was essentially all my fault, and no amount of explaining would persuade him otherwise.

"Seriously?" Janey snorts. "You're ignoring me? Wow, that's grown up of you."

I type out a quick message to my dad: please, you have to believe me. It wasn't me behind this.

I press send, holding my breath. My stomach twists. I don't think I've ever felt so nervous. But he doesn't reply. Dad rarely texts. It's a phone call or nothing for him. And he's already tried phoning me today, and I missed it. He wouldn't try again. Hell, he's probably halfway through his second bottle of wine by now, anyway.

Janey tries to talk to me as I pull my pajamas out of my wardrobe. It's surprisingly easy to ignore her. I just hum to myself as I enter our en-suite and get ready for bed.

When I emerge, teeth cleaned and face washed, Janey's watching me carefully. Her face is sullen.

"This is really mature, you know," she says. "And I can't believe what a dick you're being to me. You know, Sophie, my family has power and you know what a bitch *I can be. And if you're going to side with Courtney on all this—which was just harmless fun anyway—then you better be prepared. I'm a* Cogswell.*" She says her last name like it's royalty—except I suppose, for her and people right at the top of society it is—because they can't have their status taken away from them, whereas my family can. My father says we're barely clinging on as it is.*

Janey smiles. "And my family knows people. I'll give you until the morning to decide who you want as your bestie. Me or her."

EIGHT

Courtney

I'VE ARRANGED TO meet Zoe and Zara, after work at our local pub. Dylan's joining us a bit later, once he's finished his last meditation class.

The twins are already seated, and Zoe looks worried, her brow furrowed as she stares at her phone screen, barely acknowledging my arrival.

"She's Googling some illness again," Zara laughs.

Zoe doesn't. The blue light from the phone screen makes her olive skin look a little dull—like she is in fact coming down with something—as she peers intently at whatever website she's reading.

I press my lips together. Zoe has always been the more cautious of the twins, and since she was sixteen, she's been almost obsessed with Googling every single symptom she thinks she has. Of course she never does have anything wrong, apart from anxiety. It's all just hypochondria.

Well—apart from when she had the miscarriage last year.

She'd briefly got together with a guy she met at the gym. He was called Ben, and I'd never seen her so happy. Three months into the relationship, Zara found out she was pregnant. Ben legged it, never to be seen again since. Zara was distraught, but focused on the baby.

Then she miscarried.

Since then, we haven't seen as much of her as usual. She began staying at her house more, or saying she had to work late at the office. Our get-togethers devolved so it was just me and Zara and Dylan.

"Anyway," I say. "I've thought of a great plan for Dylan's birthday." I tell them quickly, and they both nod.

Zara works at a nightclub and reckons she can get a discount on hiring out the whole place for Dylan's birthday. Going to a club has always been something Dylan's felt he missed out on at uni—he's told me how he's got photosensitive epilepsy and anxiety about loud places and never went to one.

"And we can totally adapt the lighting and play quieter music," Zara says. "And hire our own DJ, because the guys Alec is hiring now are such sleazes."

Zoe nods. She's looking tired and overworked. She's only just got here, having driven from Plymouth where she works as an accountant. "My personal trainer is a DJ too."

"Excellent. Give me his number, and I'll phone him now," Zara says.

"Or I could ask him tonight," Zoe says.

"Fine, you do that."

I frown—there's something off between the twins today. They're both kind of sharp-tongued with each other, and that's not normal. Usually, Zara and Zoe are a united front. But looking at them now, at how tired Zoe is but how she keeps glancing at Zara, and how Zara's looking anywhere but at Zoe, I know something's wrong.

"What is it?" I ask, looking from one to the other. "Everything okay?"

"Fine," Zara says.

Zoe echoes the sentiment. But things are decidedly not fine.

Still, it's clear they don't want to talk about it to me. A few years ago, the twins had a massive falling out and refused to talk to each other, but neither would tell me what it was about. They said it was their business, and they'd sort it. They did, but I still don't know what had happened.

I look around the room, suddenly very aware of how awkward this atmosphere is.

But at that moment, Dylan arrives. I've never been so glad to see him.

He hugs all of us, and Zoe smiles at him, seems a little happier now. Though I notice she's still not happy with Zara.

My eyes fall on Dylan's open bag—and the book inside it. A bare, male torso takes up practically the whole cover.

I roll my eyes and point at the book. "Seriously? Another romance?"

He snorts, and Zara pulls the book out. I notice how relieved she looks to have something to talk about—because that's the thing. Both twins can go on and on and on—and are likely to when they're nervous or avoiding a certain subject.

"Just because you and your ace ass don't like romances doesn't mean you get to judge me," Dylan says. He folds his arms. "And it's a hell of a good writer, that one."

"I'm not judging you. Really, I'm not. And I do actually like romance. I'm not aro, just ace."

"So, what even is the problem?" Dylan's staring at me, apparently amused, one eyebrow raised.

I lean forward, take the book, and turn it over. I scan the back cover quickly. Yep. Just as I thought. "It's bully romance?" I glance up at him. "Look, I'm all for romance novels—even if they do have sex, I don't mind reading about it. But this subgenre—bully romance? I don't think that's healthy. Like why would anyone fall in love with someone who made their life hell?"

Dylan rolls his eyes. "It's not real."

"But it's sending out the wrong message," I say. "It's super unhealthy. It's—"

A phone pings. Zara's. She pulls it out of her pocket and groans.

"It's Mellie again."

"Mellie?"

"Her tutor at uni." Zoe shrugs a little.

Zara's been doing a part-time course in film and TV at the University of Exeter for the last two years. She originally studied a joint BSc of Business and Hospitality at ARU, but now she's retraining to work in the film industry.

"I have to make this film for her," Zara says. "And I want to do like a reality TV style thing—only Mellie keeps vetoing all my ideas."

"Like what?" I ask.

"Like everything I suggest—I thought about interviewing pensioners about their views on politics and reality TV, like trying to make an argument that all reality TV is political on some level. But Mellie said that sounded boring. She seems to want me to literally put on a reality-TV thing rather than a documentary about it—and then every time I come up with a reality TV idea, she says it's not original enough."

She takes back the book from me and tucks it back into Dylan's bag. The front cover snags on something and bends, and I wince. Dylan looks like he's about to cry—he's so careful with his books.

"Anyway, that's for me to worry about later," Zara says.

Zoe's posture visibly tightens at that, and I wonder if that's maybe linked to the animosity between them. And with that, that tense feeling settles back over us.

I wrack my brains for something to talk about. "You'll never guess what's happened," I say. "But Sophie Sway has moved next to me."

It's a relief to spill the beans to people who exhibit suitable emotional responses to this—horror.

"*The* Sophie Sway?" Zara raises one perfect eyebrow.

I nod. "Yup. And I can't have her living here."

"Wait, who is this girl?" Dylan asks.

I quickly explain to him—but he has heard of her before. I've mentioned Sophie quite a few times before, when talking about my St. Bridget's days. "And I'm going to make her leave. See, I've got this plan about how I'm gonna convince her that the building is haunted."

"Haunted?" Zoe snorts.

"Yes," I say. "And I've already started putting it into place."

Zara's eyes sparkle. "Need any help?"

Even Zoe's looking interested, too. Maybe this can be something they'll bond over again?

"Oh, for sure. I'm still fine-tuning the details."

"Just don't do anything that'll get you in actual trouble," Zoe says, ever the practical one. "We don't need to be picking you up from the police station or anything."

She laughs, and then Dylan's asking if we want another round of drinks.

"I'll just have an orange juice," I say, thinking of my mother. She may be completely wrong about me being an alcoholic, but it's not hard to realize why she's so worried. My father practically drank himself to death when I was six. He'd had liver problems for years, but he'd never give up the drink.

Dylan heads toward the bar, chanting our orders under his breath. He always does that. Says he has the worst memory.

"Oh my goodness," Zara say. "I've just had the craziest idea." She takes a dramatically deep breath. "You and Sophie—your rivalry. That's the perfect topic for my film. Mellie's going to love it, I'm sure."

"Uh, what do you mean?" I ask.

The twins both look at me.

"So, you know I need to make this reality TV film? And I want to look at something from different points of view? Well, what about revisiting the old rivalry between you and Sophie? Oh, oh, oh! We need to make it into a game—audiences love games. It can be a competition, and you'd get to embarrass her loads."

I frown. "But she'd be trying to embarrass me too?"

"But you'd win, easily," Zara says. "Anyway, don't you want to do this? Wipe that smug smile off her face, once and for all?"

I have to admit it does sound rather appealing. "What kind of things would make up the game though?"

"Pranks," Zara says, not missing a beat. "Like what you did in Years Nine and Ten? Only this would be the ultimate prank war."

A grin spreads across my face.

Zoe swallows hard. "Sophie would have to agree to this."

"She will," Zara says. "I mean, given everything that happened in Year Eleven, she owes Courtney. And you want to do this, right?"

"Beat Sophie at a game and humiliate her?" I snort. "Of course."

NINE

Sophie

"I KNEW YOU'D see sense," Janey says as she hands me a takeaway cup of hot chocolate from the café down the road. Then she links her arm in mine and leads me forward.

I make a noncommittal noise. I didn't want to make amends with Janey—at least, not as soon as this—but I spoke to my father this morning, and he said I was being silly, choosing the scholarship girl over a powerful girl like Janey. Apparently, he's got some golf tournament coming up where he'll also be discussing business, and Janey's uncles will be there too. He can't risk my falling out with Janey having a knock-on effect on his business. So, this morning, I apologized to Janey, even if it made my stomach curdle. Janey had sniffed loudly when I'd done it, and told me that it 'wasn't cool' that I'd 'dobbed her in' to Mr. Tawse like that.

"We're supposed to be friends, and friends look out for each other," she'd said, haughtily.

I'd groveled until I'd felt sick to my stomach, but now Janey smiles at me as she looks across at me. My arm is in hers, and we're drinking hot chocolate together.

It's Saturday, and she says we'll meet Rebecca and Stacey in town at the cinema.

The weather's good for once too—not too cold, and not too warm— but it doesn't feel like it will be a good day. Not when my stomach is churning like this, and the hot chocolate's just too sweet. I bet it's got loads of calories.

It doesn't take long to meet Rebecca and Stacey outside the cinema. Janey makes some stupid joke and they both laugh, so then I laugh too, remembering my father's words—how I must do everything and anything to get back in Janey's good books. So, I'm laughing at whatever Janey's just said, when Courtney and the twins round the corner.

Courtney clearly sees me laughing with Janey, and the look on her face is like a kick in the gut for making me realize that things are never going to be good between us again—because our rivalry was fun. We constantly tried to outdo each other, but we respected each other too. We had each other's backs. Like in the cross-country competition when I fell down, she helped me up, even though it made her slower. And right before the spelling bee, she was upset because she couldn't find her lucky necklace, so I let her borrow mine—even though it wasn't a lucky necklace at all. But giving it to her had lit up her eyes, and she'd given me the warmest hug then.

We were never quite friends, but we weren't enemies. We didn't hate each other. We didn't avoid each other. We didn't look at each other with eyes dark and brimming. The rivalry was healthy for both of us. Pushing us to be our best. After all, a rival is a benchmark for improvement.

But it's not like that now.

And Janey—Janey, who my father made me choose—has ruined that.

"Let's go in," Rebecca says.

"Yes," Janey says, pulling me closer to her. "Let's go. Come on, Soph. We'll sit at the back."

TEN
Sophie

MY HAND SHAKES as I unlock the door—did the knocking at it sound heavy and masculine? Like Adam?

Part of me wants to just hide, wait for whoever it is to go away. But I've got a delivery due. I ordered some books with Amazon Prime yesterday—books on writing craft—and if this is them, I need to answer the door.

The door swings open, and it's not my delivery. Instead, I stare at the three women at the door. Courtney, and a pair of beautiful identical twins who have to be Zara and Zoe, all grown up. Seriously? Courtney's brought back-up here?

I shift my weight from foot to foot.

"Hi," Zara says—or at least I think it's her. She's got a small scar on her forehead, and I'm pretty sure she's the twin with that, otherwise it's hard to tell them apart. "Oh, is this Sergeant Ginger Paws?" She coos at the cat who's somewhere behind me, and then she sidles past me.

I turn, my gaze following her as she sits on the sofa.

"Wait, what are you doing?" I look at Zara then back to Zoe and Courtney. At least those two haven't just walked in.

They're still standing awkwardly at the front door. Yep, Zoe was always the more cautious twin. And wow, those are some huge bags under her eyes.

"Sorry," Courtney mutters. "Look, I think it's best if Zara explains?"

"Yeah, so, yesterday, we had this crazy idea," Zara says as Sergeant climbs all over her. "And it would be amazing to do it." She gives a very wicked grin, one that has the hairs on the back of my neck standing on edge.

"Wait, what?" I say. I frown. "What's going on?"

"Sorry to barge in like this," Courtney says, and I swear she glares at Zara. She smooths down her clothes—a shapeless dress with a skirt of a very respectable length. Has she just finished work? "But we need to make a film."

"A film?" I stare at them, then take a step back.

"Well, *I* need to make one," Zara says. "Oh my goodness— yes, Kitty. You're so cute. Anyway, Sophie. I'm doing a degree in film production, and I've got to make a film that's reality TV, and we were wondering if you'd be interested in a star role in it?"

A star role? I stare at her. "Me?" It's no secret that these three hated me at school, so I just don't get it now. "What's the catch? I mean… This is all weird."

Or maybe they recognize that I'm easily the most beautiful out of the four of us? Because I realize I definitely *am* as I assess the three of them. I mean, Courtney still appears to have a phobia of makeup or indeed making any sort of effort at all. Her dark brown hair is piled up high on her head in a messy knot and the dress is baggy. Zara and Zoe, though they are beautiful are quite short, and I'm definitely skinnier. And sure, I may not be a model now, but I still take pride in my appearance.

"Okay," Zara says. "This is about you and Courtney, and the rivalry you had at school. And I want to film something fun too, something engaging. And then we had the best idea." She glances at Courtney and gives her the thumbs-up.

Courtney looks a little bewildered but steps closer to me. "We continue our rivalry now—I mean, we're living next door to each other, practically. And we can make a game out of it."

"A game?" I raise my eyebrows. In my pocket, I feel my phone vibrate.

I inhale sharply—the vibration means a text message. I've turned all other notifications to silent at the moment. Only texts vibrate, and there's only one person who'd be texting me.

I try not to think about Adam, try not to think about what he could be saying, threatening. I mean, he's not *actually* going to turn up here. He was never interested in my family— whenever I mentioned Victoria and Martin, as my only sort-of relatives, Adam always yawned and said they didn't count as they weren't blood relatives. I'm pretty sure he doesn't know where they live, where I am now.

"Yes, because that would make it super fun, too," Zara says. "I'll interview you both at different times, and then we'll film your pranks."

"Pranks?" I ask. My breathing is fast, and I'm trying to concentrate on this conversation—and not the unread text on my phone—but I've become so invested in concentrating on Zara and Courtney and Zoe that I'm barely taking anything in.

"Well, yeah, I mean you can't actually do anything that will majorly hurt the other person. But this would pretty much cover all the criteria for my film. I can interview you each about your school-days' rivalry and about how you feel now, turning it into a game. And we can do the filming across the next month. You want to be an actor right, Sophie?"

I blink. "How do you know that?" Because being an actor *is* my dream—only it's one I don't really talk about anymore. Not since Adam pointed out that when people hear a former model wants to be an actor, they assume the model just thinks they'll be cast because they're pretty. And he did have a point—I've heard a few people referring to it as cheating too, getting a way into the acting industry because you're beautiful and a former model, rather than because you're actually good at acting.

And I love acting—but I'm scared too. Scared that people will just see me as only a former model. A blonde with an amazing figure. And they'll think I haven't really worked for any acting jobs, not like other actors.

And then there's my fear of failure, of actually being bad at something. I'm self-conscious now—I have been since my breakup. Well, before then. Since meeting Adam. He really eroded my self-esteem and confidence. I've always wanted to run my own business, alongside act and write, but every suggestion I came up with for a business idea, he told me was stupid. He kept saying I didn't have to work. He could bring money in, and in any case, I had my inheritance. My inheritance that he was swiftly making his way through…

"Read your LinkedIn page," Zara says in a very dismissive tone, and I frown—I'd put about my acting dream on there? "You follow a lot of studios." Zara pets Sergeant a little more. "So, this is perfect for all of us. And I can pay you in chocolate."

I wrinkle my nose. Alarm bells ring in my head. "I can't have chocolate."

"You can't have chocolate?" Courtney stares at me. "You loved it at school."

I press my lips together. I still love chocolate—but chocolate's bad, and no matter how many therapists tell me that food has no moral value, and that it's categorizations like that which often lead to feelings of guilt over eating certain things, and then onto eating disorders, I can't dismiss that line of thinking. It's so ingrained into me. It started when I was fourteen or so. It got worse at university. Even worse when I was with Adam for those few years. And now it's just... I don't know what it is. But it's there.

"Wine?" Zara suggests. "I mean, we're being nice giving you something anyway. With the way you outed Courtney like that, you kind of owe her."

I glance at Courtney, see the tips of her ears reddening. There's still a sadness in her eyes—I can see that. And sure, it wasn't me who did, it was Janey—but I should've been better. I should've dumped Janey's toxic ass and showed Courtney that our friendship, if that's what you could've called it, was more important. Because Janey dropped me as soon as we left school. She no longer had to be civil to me, and she took Rebecca and Stacey with her. I was left friendless, alone.

"So, are you in?" Zara gives me the look—the one that tells me I have no choice. And maybe it's not a bad thing?

I nod. "I'm in."

"Don't look so sad about it then," Zara says. "I need this to be fun."

ELEVEN

Courtney

THIS IS WEIRD. So weird. Making the rivalry into a game is just… Well, I can't think of any other word for it than 'weird,' I mean, it's nerve-wracking knowing that upstairs, Sophie is plotting something. I'm still no way near comfortable around her—not after how things turned out between us at school. I mean, she'd made such an effort to tell me it was all Janey, and not her, yet just a day or so later, she was back to being best friends with that girl.

No, Sophie is a viper. And I'm not sure agreeing to this prank war was a good idea now. I mean, Zara was particular about it needing to be pranks and not actual things that could hurt either of us. But I've already been burnt by Sophie before, and I'm incredibly nervous now. Just what could she be planning?

And what am I going to plan as my prank to play on her?

I stare at my notepad. I only work mornings on Thursdays, and I went over to the club to finalize the set-up for Dylan's party tonight, and then headed back here. I've been jotting a few ideas of things I could do to prank Sophie. Top of the list is continuing the 'Make Sophie think the building is haunted' idea. That's easily the strongest idea on the list—I mean swapping salt and sugar around at her house would just be pathetic, not that it would even be easy to do if I'm not invited in, because I'm not breaking and entering—so I've been trying to think about other ways I can make her really think the house is haunted.

I spend a good few hours reading up on signs of ghosts—everything from cold spots in the air and drafts, to spikes in EMF readings, and hearing someone call your name. While the latter I could do through the ceiling, like with the tapping, the rest all require access to the house. And Zoe was quick to point out that there should be a 'no breaking and entering' rule. If we need to go in the other's apartment, that has to be arranged. Or we should do pranks from afar or online—which will have to do for Sophie, as there's no way I'm inviting her in here. All prank plans must also be vetted by Zara first to ensure it's not going too far—and when we're carrying them out, we need to do some vlog-style filming to capture it all, if Zara's not already there filming it. And then on each Friday for the next three weeks, we'll meet too, so Sophie and I can be interviewed officially for the film.

I almost can't believe this is happening.

Zara okayed my haunting plan, and so I take out my camera now and do a quick thirty second piece, telling the viewer what I'm planning. I feel incredibly self-conscious though, talking to the camera like this, and part of me almost feels like Sophie automatically is listening in, somehow.

I busy myself for another half an hour—until it's time to leave for Dylan's party. Zara and Jack had got most of it ready by the time I arrived after my morning at work, but I'd put the finishing touches on, and Zoe's bringing the food tonight.

I head out, and try to put Sophie right to the back of my mind.

"Daddy, come on!" Kayla yells, pulling at Dylan's hand.

She toddles forward in the dark with so much enthusiasm she nearly face-plants the ground, but Dylan and I pull her up just in time. Her face is flushed with excitement, and the only signs of her earlier tantrum are the faint ghost tracks of tears down her face. As soon as I arrived at their apartment and told Kayla in stage whispers that we had an exciting surprise for her dad planned, and that I needed her help in getting Dylan there 'without him suspecting anything,' she was game. She stopped screaming about Charlotte at the daycare—a kid she doesn't like, because Charlotte bites everyone—and was clearly delighted that I trusted her with the secret.

Now, the three of us are heading toward Angelic, the club Zara works at.

"I can't imagine why we're going here," Dylan says with a slight role of his eyes that's meant just for me.

"Because we are!" Kayla smiles and picks up her pace so she's practically running.

We get to the door, and I push it open.

Kayla pulls Dylan straight in and—

"Surprise!" everyone shouts.

An orange light floods the entrance foyer and then everyone's smiling and wishing Dylan happy birthday while Kayla's asking where the cupcakes are.

"This way," Zoe says to her, with a smile, taking Kayla's hand in her own. To be honest, I think Kayla's just excited about being out in the evening.

"Oh my god!" Dylan's eyes look a deep amber under the orange light, and I can tell he's seen the first 'stop.'

The sign is for Puerto Rico, and Jack was largely in charge of that one. He's done a pretty good job too. Impressive. He's got a bowl of some sort of mashed plantain—which Zara said had way too much garlic in—and one of those banners showing vividly blue sea, an idyllic beach, and some sort of expensive looking hotel. To the side of the banner is a fake palm tree, one of the inflatable ones. It's been at the bottom of my wardrobe for ages, ever since I bought it during Freshers' week at uni.

"Come and take a walk down the San Juan streets," Jack says, indicating the walkway. We made it out of some flimsy art gallery walls that Zoe found at her office—she said no one knew why they were there—and she'd had fun painting the street art directly onto it.

"This is amazing," Dylan says.

Kayla returns, half a cupcake crammed into her mouth, the rest smeared down her dress. She reaches for Dylan's hand. "Tour!"

We've decked out the whole of the club as a travel around the world, picking out various places that we know Dylan's always wanted to go but never has been able to due to his illness.

And thus, we are traveling the world today, stopping at all the 'cool and important' places, as Kayla excitedly tells anyone who will listen.

Afterward, Dylan takes Kayla back home, leaving me, the twins, and Jack in the club.

"I think it was a success," Jack murmurs. He clinks his drink against mine. He's got champagne, but I've got apple juice. That promise to my mum and all.

Really, it's ridiculous that she thinks I'm an alcoholic—I mean, I get why she's nervous, given what happened to Dad. But this is me. I don't even drink more than the average person. She just happened to see me super drunk one day, and she jumped to conclusions, picturing me like that every evening.

Still, I suppose it's easy for her to do, when she lived that nightmare with Dad for years.

TWELVE

Courtney

THE STREETS ARE busy, packed with last-minute Christmas shoppers, and I weave through the crowds. I need to get back to St. Bridget's. I can't afford to miss the curfew on the last day of term.

I turn left and—

"Courtney?" a woman says.

It takes me a moment to realize it's Ms. Trenway. She looks different—her hair's short now, and she's not wearing any makeup. She also looks like she's aged ten years in the last two months.

None of us have seen her at school since the assembly. There've been rumors that she was suspended due to the 'relationship' with me—which is a load of bullshit—but I've also heard rumors that she resigned, that she started her own commune, and (my favorite) that she got scouted by some talent agency. Because Ms. Trenway is awesome at acting—everyone knows that.

"Courtney, I'm so happy I bumped into you," she says, gesturing for me to come closer.

I step to the side.

"I've been wanting to know how you are since those bullies outed you like that." Genuine concern fills her eyes. "And I know I shouldn't really *be talking to you, you know, fueling the rumors and all that, but I've been concerned and I just want you to know that you can talk to me at any time, if you want to."*

"Uh, thanks," I say. I smile, but this whole thing feels weird.

She fishes in her bag for a card. "Here's my number."

I take the card and turn it over. Simone Mitchell, freelance actor. "You've changed your name?"

"Got married," she says, smiling. "Last month. Only good thing to happen recently."

"Oh, wow. Uh, congratulations. So, you're really an actor now too?" I stare at her.

And her whole face lights up. "I was before—I had small parts alongside teaching. My agent has been great, getting me more auditions since…" She shrugs. "I do miss teaching though. I miss seeing all you girls, and I'm saddened to think about everything that's going on at St. Bridget's in the wake of that assembly. Cora—uh, Miss Aylott—told me that there have been some rumors spreading about you. But Courtney, you must give me a call if you want to chat any time, if you need a friend."

"Thanks," I say.

"The weirdest thing happened out there." I pull my coat off and throw it over the chair by my desk.

"Oh yeah?" Zara looks up from where she's sprawled on my bed.

Zoe's sitting on her bed, so I take Zara's—I don't know why she constantly lounges on mine and not her own, anyway.

"I saw Ms. Trenway. Out shopping. By Debenhams."

"Ms. Trenway?" Zara's eyebrows shoot up.

Even Zoe looks up from her phone.

"And?" Zara prompts.

"She's called Mrs. Mitchell now. She got married. And she just wanted to check I was okay," I say, leaning back onto Zara's unmade bed. "She gave me her card—she's an actor now. Proper actor, I reckon. Mentioned an agent and everything. Anyway, I want to get to the canteen before they close. I haven't eaten yet."

The clock tells me I've got ten minutes to grab something, and Zara says she'll come with me.

"Anything to get away from old misery guts," she mutters once we've left the room and the door is shut.

I wince, hoping Zoe didn't hear that. "What's going on?"

"Nothing more than Zoe being her usual hypochondriac self." Zara laughs. "Seriously, I don't get why she's convinced she's got something. Why would she even want to be ill? It just doesn't make sense. And you'd think she'd realize that she can't have something when I'm okay."

"What?" I squint at her.

"We're identical twins, dummy. If she's got some horrible genetic disorder—which is her current obsession—then I've got it too. And her anxiety may be giving her symptoms, but I've got none. God, that should reassure her, but it doesn't."

"Well," I say, "that doesn't mean she can't get something you haven't got. Like, catch a virus. Like Lyme disease or something? That's environmental. Ticks and that."

Zara snorts. "Don't give her that idea. She'll latch onto it quicker than you can say... I don't know what you could say, but honestly, don't humor her. There's nothing wrong with her."

THIRTEEN

Courtney

"LIGHTS, CAMERA, ACTION!" Zara yells, giggling. Wine sloshes out of the glass she's holding as she waves it about.

It's just me and the twins here, at Zara's apartment, and I'd be lying if I said I wasn't contemplating having a drink. Fridays are always hectic at work. And a drink does sound good.

I mean, Mum wouldn't know… but I am volunteering later at the center. Manning the phones until ten.

Then again, I don't want to have to lie to her.

I settle back on the sofa, watching Zara's spilling wine with concern. When she's drunk, she's not careful. But when she's sober, she freaks out over any stains on her precious sofa. I remember one time when our extended family visited from Singapore and two of the young children spilled their dinner all over Zara's dress. She was so upset. She's not going to be happy later.

I glance at Zoe then back to Zara.

"Are you filming?" Zara stage-whispers to her sister, then hiccups. She laughs and reaches for the half-empty wine bottle— of which she's the sole consumer—and tops up her glass.

Zoe, behind the camera, nods. "Of course I'm filming." Her voice is neutral and slow, like each word is poised carefully on the edge of a precipice. I still don't understand what is going on between the twins.

"Okay!" Zara shrieks, and she scoots closer to me on the sofa. "Come on, Zoe, move closer. We need close-ups of this conversation."

Zoe brings the camera closer—a little too close for my liking as my acne is going to show up on the camera perfectly now. I need to go back to the doctor about this—the breakouts have been terrible the last few months. I had terrible acne as a teenager, but it cleared up when I was around twenty. Only now, six years later, it's back with a vengeance. Maybe something hormonal is going on.

"So, Courtney, tell us about Sophie," Zara says. "This is where...where we want to get an idea for what she was like at school. And we want juicy details about the two of you! And what better way to overcome a rivalry than to turn it to a prank contest." She turns to the camera and pouts. "We'll be following Courtney and Sophie across the next month. Each week, they'll plan and carry out a new prank. Our panel of judges—Zoe Davenport-Grey, Jack Wallander, and Dylan Cosgrove—will decide on the winner for each week, with the final week being double-points. At the end of the month, we'll announce the Queen of Pranks!"

Zara does a mini cheer all on her own before turning back to me. "So, you've told us all about the rivalry between you and Sophie at school. But what about as adults?"

"We've not really spoken—I mean, only a couple times since she moved next door."

"So, do you think you two can ever be friends?"

I shrug. "Unlikely. But I guess we'll see how this game goes."

"Indeed, we will," Zara says. "Let's start playing Queen of Pranks."

"Hello, this is Tabitha speaking at Places for Aces."

"Hi, uh, I wanted to ask about whether I could be asexual," a deep voice says. "My girlfriend says I must be because I'm never into getting intimate, and she's annoyed that I didn't tell her I was ace to start with—but I don't think I am, yet she says that's the only explanation for not being into sex when I haven't been abused. Which she keeps asking me to check, and yeah, she says I've deceived her."

"Okay, so firstly, not liking sex or being sex-repulsed doesn't *equal* being asexual," I say. "They're two separate things. Asexuals can be sex-repulsed, but not all are. Some are sex-neutral and some are sex-positive. And allos can be sex-repulsed, too, just as they can also be neutral or positive. Asexuality is to do with whether you experience sexual attraction, it's not based on whether you like sex or are repulsed by it."

"Okay." He sounds like he's frowning. "So, I mean, I never *want* to have sex—like, I mean, I *can* do it. But I find it… It's… I just don't want to. Like, I'd rather drive pins into my eyes sometimes than do it. And I feel so bad saying this, but half the time I just try to think of any excuse that means we don't do it. I just… She thinks I must've been abused and it's not really something I can just ask my mum. And… well…" He trails off.

I wait for him to speak again, but when he doesn't, I say, "Hey, that's a valid way to feel. It doesn't mean there's anything wrong with you or that you've repressed abuse or anything."

"So, you think I *am* asexual?"

"Well," I say. "It sounds like you're possibly sex-repulsed. But do you experience sexual attraction?"

The line crackles a bit. "I don't know—I get confused. I've tried looking it up, and I just… I don't understand the differences between sexual attraction and sexual desire and sex drive. Because, look, if you ask me if I *want* to have sex, then it's a no. I never really feel like I want to do it. But if I get…uh, stimulated… then sometimes I do like the feeling of it—but I mean, it doesn't make any difference if it's just me there or if it's my girlfriend…doing it. But because my body seems to like it, I mean, it reacts and everything, so I get confused— especially when I haven't felt like I wanted to have sex to start with. Because it's like my body's acting differently to how I feel. Sorry, I want to say more, but this is really embarrassing."

"It's okay," I say. This conversation's mild compared to some I've had. "Honestly, don't worry. This is a safe place to talk. Would you like to continue what you were saying?"

"Okay." He clears his throat. "Well, sometimes I feel I need sexual release? But I'd rather just take care of it on my own if that happens. I don't like sex, and my girlfriend says it's really affecting her confidence as it means she's not attractive enough for me, and then she insults my manhood. I rarely initiate it, and when I do, it's because I know she wants it. Shit, it's such a mess—you know? And I love her, but I just… Sometime I think I can just put up with it. Like maybe I should just do that. Or see a therapist to work out why I don't like sex."

"Okay, well it very much sounds like you may be on the ace spectrum," I say. "There are quite a lot of aces who experience some sort of sex drive, but they still don't experience sexual attraction to anyone. Would you say it's fair to say that's what you're describing?"

"I'm not sure. Like, how can you have a sex drive though if you don't have sexual attraction? I'm still really confused."

"So, your libido—your sex drive—is about the physical relief that you get from sex, okay? So, that can be done on your own. Sexual attraction is about whether you're sexually attracted to other people. So, someone who's ace experiences little or no sexual attraction to others, but they can also have a high sex drive. One doesn't negate the other. A lot of aces masturbate."

"Well, I guess that does sound like me. God, Ashley's going to be thrilled."

"Is Ashley your girlfriend?" I ask.

"Yep."

"Well, I think you need to sit down with her properly and talk about it all. Because you've clearly expressed to me that you often don't want to have sex—yet you feel like you have to, because you're worried about how she'll feel? But I'm worried about the effect that's having on you." I press my lips together. I mean, what he's saying is pretty much sexual coercion, but I always feel nervous telling callers that. I don't want to upset them, and one time when I did tell a woman that, she got really annoyed with me for apparently trying to paint her boyfriend in a negative light. I focus back on the conversation. "If you're constantly feeling under pressure to have sex and you're repulsed by it, I worry how that's going to affect not only you but also your relationship with your girlfriend. There's a chance it could breed resentment, and so I really think you need to discuss this. If you'd like, you're welcome to bring her into the call now?"

He makes a non-committal sound. "I don't think that's a good idea."

"Why not?"

"Like, she's not said it outright, but I'm sure she is hoping this can just be easily fixed. Like if I was abused, like she keeps saying, then I could just get therapy and be normal again. But I'm worried that if she knows that I actually probably *am* asexual that she'll just leave me."

I lean back in my chair. "It sounds like you're under a lot of stress at the moment and you're obviously worried, but I have to say that if she would leave you because you're ace, then it sounds like she's not the best partner for you."

"I don't want to lose her," he says. "I love her. And I'm really scared she's just going to say she's had enough. I mean, she's made it clear she needs sex, and I'm struggling with it. But I just don't know how to make it work for both of us."

"Well, there are ways to make ace/allo relationships work," I say. "And it comes down to communication and being respectful of your partner's boundaries. But, I'm sorry to say, it sounds like she's not being respectful of your boundaries. And she does seem to be using an element of guilt against you—making you feel guilty for not wanting sex with her."

"Yeah," he says, his voice flat. He exhales very loudly. "I guess I'll think about it for a while."

"Okay," I say, rubbing the back of my neck. My bee tattoo feels like it's moving, like the bee is fluttering. "You're welcome to call back any time. You can either ask for me again or speak to one of our other call-handlers."

"What's your name again?"

"Tabitha."

"Right. Well, thanks, Tabitha."

And with that, he's gone. The line's dead and I stare at the computer screen in front of me for a few moments, wondering if we'll ever hear from him—or his girlfriend—again.

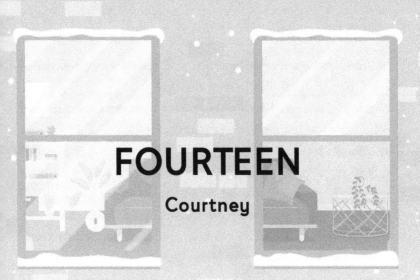

FOURTEEN

Courtney

"IS THIS REALLY a good idea?" Mum asks, her voice a little foggy due to interference on the line. She doesn't have a mobile, just still uses that really old-fashioned landline, and half the time I can barely hear her. "Think how upset you were as a teenager, when Sophie and her friends did what they did."

"I know, I know." I breathe deeply and continue kneading the dough. I've got Mum on speakerphone, my phone propped up on the windowsill, and I'm attempting to make my own bread. I mean, I've been trying for a good while—at least several months, every Saturday morning—and I'm still struggling with the texture. I actually phoned Mum for guidance on it, but of course our conversation meandered toward Zara's project.

"I just don't want you getting hurt, again," Mum says.

"It's already started," I say. "Zara's really into this whole game thing, and it'll be fine. Honest."

Mum doesn't sound convinced, no matter how much I try to explain that this isn't like at St. Bridget's. It's strange, she was all for saying Sophie will have grown up last time we called, but now she's worried. But I try to reassure you.

Here, I feel like I'll have more control in the situation. And what's the worse that Sophie can do? Out me again? Dylan and the twins already know, as does Sally. The only other person I talk to regularly is Mrs. Dalton, but she's a cherub, and I can't imagine her being acephobic or anything.

Not like how people were at school. After that assembly, so many people made snide comments and demanded to know about my sex life and why I was like this. It's one thing that annoys me about being ace—so many people automatically assume they can ask you deeply personal questions.

After the call with Mum, I head out to meet Dylan and the twins. Dylan lives near me, only a couple blocks away, and I join up with him outside his building and give him Kayla's birthday present for tomorrow.

"What do you think of this?" he asks, flashing his hot-pink nails in front of my face. "Kayla persuaded me."

I laugh and peer at his very messy nails. "And she did the painting too?"

"She did. Right before my mum came to get her. She's taking her to the zoo. She wants to paint the tigers' claws pink too."

We're still laughing about it when we get to the pub where we're meeting the twins, but as soon as we arrive, I can tell something's wrong. Zara's sitting alone, her face a strange ashen color as she stares straight ahead.

"Hey," I say. "Where's Zoe?"

Tears well up in Zara's eyes, and she tries to blink them away, but then they're overflowing.

"Whoa," Dylan says, scooping her up into a hug. He wraps his arms tightly around her and I can see now that Zara's trembling.

"It's... God. She's gonna hate me for telling you."

"Telling us what?" I shift my weight to my other foot and frown. "What's happened?"

"She's... Oh, I was such a bitch to her, telling her before she was being super dramatic, but..."

"Slow down," I say. "Just speak calmly. Because I have no idea what you're talking about."

Zara nods. "Zoe's been diagnosed with endometriosis."

My eyes widen. *Holy sheep.* I've heard about that. Heard it's one of the most painful diseases around and that in severe cases organs can get fused together.

Dylan is frowning. "What is it?"

"Womb lining growing in places that it shouldn't," Zara says. "Zoe told me a while ago she was going to see a doctor because her periods had become really painful. Like, you know she was always complaining about that at school? Saying she thought she was dying every time she got her period?"

I nod. "I remember."

"Well, she told me that it was really bad—and you know before, we thought she was being sick on the days of her period because she'd worked herself up into a state from her anxiety and hypochondria? Well, it turns out that was a symptom."

"It was?"

"She said that's what the doctor told her. And then since she had the miscarriage, it's been even worse. I just... I really thought it was nothing, all those years ago." She winces. "I laughed at her and told her it was a normal amount of pain she had, because mine was normal. And I really believed we were the same, being identical and that. I thought she just had a low pain threshold or something. I had no idea there actually was something."

I frown. "Was this why you two have been a bit off with each other?"

She nods. "And she phoned me in floods of tears last night. She'd had an MRI last week, and she saw the gynecologist yesterday—who's confirmed it looks like endometriosis."

"Confirmed it *looks like it?*" Dylan frowns. "So, does that mean it is or it isn't?"

Zara shakes her head. "I don't know. Zoe said something about surgery being the only way to tell if it is that, like when they remove it. But she said the MRI scan showed the endometriosis was in her bowel as well. Oh, and she's got to have a lap—what was the word? Lap-something-scopy." She looks at me. "Does that sound right?"

I shrug. "I don't know."

"When's it happening?" Dylan asks.

"I don't know. She was in such a state."

"Is she meeting us here?" I ask.

Zara shakes her head. "She's gone to see Mum. I said I'd go with her, but she didn't want me there—she's never said that to me before. We used to do everything together—and now I've ruined it. Truly ruined things. Honestly, we've never fallen out like this."

I pat her back lightly. "It'll be okay. It has to be."

Zara swallows hard. "There's no cure for it. And everything I've been reading says it can just get worse and worse." Her voice is a fraction too high—it sounds closer to Zoe, when she's fretting over illness, convinced she has something serious.

Only she has.

"There'll be ways to manage it though," Dylan says. "There has to be. We'll find something. We'll do something to help."

FIFTEEN

Sophie

"SERIOUSLY?" JANEY RAISES her eyebrows at me. "You're wearing that?"

"What's wrong with it?" I glare at her, as if I can actually get her to step back with the power of my vision.

But she steps closer and runs a finger over the left shoulder strap of my dress. "You wore it last year?"

"And what's wrong with that?" I keep my tone even and fold my arms. "Exactly—nothing."

She frowns. "Sophie, we have appearances to maintain. People look to us to set the standard—only you're falling way below the acceptable bar now."

I let out a frustrated sigh. "Janey, for God's sake, it's just a dress."

"A dress for the ball."

"Exactly, a stupid school ball. Nothing more than that."

But Janey's shaking her head. "You'll have to borrow one of mine. There's a cream taffeta one in my wardrobe. Wear that. It might be a bit tight on you, but it'll have to do. I can't believe you didn't tell me before that you didn't have a dress."

"Because I have a dress," I say.

She shakes her head. "You know, it's a good job we're friends. Where would you be without me?"

With Courtney, I want to reply. Because if Janey wasn't here, she'd never have done that stupid PowerPoint slide and outed Courtney or got Ms. Trenway suspended. And I'd still be talking to Courtney—maybe even actually friends by now. My heart warms at that thought, but Janey's over by her wardrobe now. She chucks a bundle of fabric at me.

"Wear it."

"No, I don't think I want to change out of this one." I finger the hem of the bodice carefully. My mother chose this dress.

"Nonsense, Sophie," Janey says. "We're the popular girls here, and there are so many who would try to usurp us in a heartbeat. We can't let that happen, so you have to follow the rules. Now, put this on and don't mention your stupid dress ever again."

"Have you made up with Janey?" Dad asks the next day, on our weekly call.

I nod, then say, "Yes," when I realize he can't see me.

I breathe out hard, and my eyes unfocus a little. My head's hazy. I haven't eaten, and I've barely drunk anything today. I like the haziness of it—it sort of makes me feel like I'm floating.

"Good. We're very proud of you. The whole family is."

I try not to let those words affect me, but I can't help it. He's always putting so much pressure on me—and now he's even deciding who I can and can't be friends with.

Exhaustion weighs me down. There was a time, before, when I'd fight this, be more assertive. But now everything almost feels too difficult.

It's just easier to go along with what everyone else wants.

SIXTEEN

Sophie

"SO," ZARA SAYS, raising an eyebrow. "You've had time now to come up with the ultimate prank and you've even called us in to film it—so, drum roll please." She smiles, and looks slightly drunk. In a stage-whisper, she says, "Jack said he can add the sound of a drumroll here." She clears her throat, and then speaks in that over-excited exuberant voice again: "So, Sophie Sway, please tell us what your round one prank on Courtney Davenport will be?"

I sit rigidly in the chair, keeping my back straight. One waxed leg is folded over the other, and I know I'm angling my best side toward the camera. Some guy named Dylan is behind it, but other than telling me his name I don't know who he is. He also doesn't seem to like me much, if the number of times he's shot glares at me is anything to go by.

No matter how hard I try, I can't not be aware of my posture. It's weird having Zara and this guy in here—Victoria's flat—and it's just making me all the more self-conscious. That and I'm nervous anyway because the door's unlocked. But it would've looked weird to them if I'd locked them inside here, with me, wouldn't it?

I realize Zara's waiting for me to speak.

"So, as you all know, I also write. I'm a girl of many talents." I wince as I hear how that sounds—all big-headed. "And I'll be writing Courtney in as the villain of my story." I grin widely, waiting for them to laugh and congratulate me on my awesome idea. Because the prank has to be harmless. But neither is looking enthusiastic. Zara's mouth has dropped open, and Dylan looks about as unenthusiastic as possible. "It'll just be an extra draft," I clarify. "Not the one that's going to the printers." I laugh. "Ha, imagine that!"

Zara frowns and leans closer to me. "Well, uh, that's great. Perfect for round one. Starting with baby steps. I like it." She looks at Dylan. "And cut."

Dylan grunts as he presses something on the camera. It's on a massive tripod set up in my living room. Well, Victoria's living room. Apparently, they had trouble getting the tripod up the stairs and the lift is out of order. Not that I would know—I always take the stairs. Exercise is preferable—and I need to exercise. Exercise keeps you healthy. Everyone knows that.

But my mind darkens as I think about what Adam said: how I needed to make sure I stayed in shape. He didn't want a fat girlfriend.

It was only a few weeks after we'd moved in together, when he found out the extent of my food issues, that he really began laying into me. He encouraged it, goaded me, tracked my calories, constantly telling me that soon I'd be a size 0, and then *Wouldn't you look so hot? A model who's a size 0!* But he also began to complain about my routines, calling them ridiculous because I was doing those rather than spending time with him. But it's not ridiculous to go swimming three times a week and for a run each morning. It's not ridiculous to go to the gym each evening. It's not ridiculous to have fasting days.

A year later, and he was getting angry at me regularly. Adam just didn't respect my need for routine. He told me I was a control freak, even though I never once tried to force him to stick to my routines. They were always only just for me. I weathered it all as best as I could, for as long as we could. But then last month we ended up having this massive argument, and he stormed out the flat, all blood-shot eyes and heavy sighs. And I knew he had a bit of a gambling problem—but I never expected him to bet the *flat* that evening, no matter how upset he was.

"So, remember to film as you're writing Courtney into your book," Zara says. "Like, just on your phone is fine. We'll edit it all so it's like home-camera footage from amateurs, that sort of thing, so don't worry too much about quality. So long as we can see it, it's good. The main talk of the show will be the interviews each Friday anyway, and plus we'll properly film the final pranks too. The *grand* pranks."

"Huh," Dylan says.

Zara turns to look at him. "What?"

"Nothing," he says. "You're just really into this. That's all." He clears his throat. "Well, I better be going. Got to get ready for class."

"Class?" I ask. "Are you studying too?"

He shakes his head. "I teach meditation. Meditation class."

"Oh," I say, and I think of the meditation app on my phone and how I just can't get it to work or can't quite get in the zone. Maybe I need an in-person class. Only Dylan's already leaving now, and he doesn't seem that friendly toward me anyway.

Once Dylan and Zara have both left, and I've locked the door and triple-checked it, and fed Sergeant, I set about writing Courtney in as the villain of my story. It's a dark thriller about a girl who stalks her ex-girlfriend, and doing a find and replace on names is easy enough. For good measure I add a couple of descriptions of Courtney too: her olive skin and her black hair and how her eyes are so bright and full of life that they just seem to sparkle. And that way she has of holding herself too—it just makes her look so effortlessly confident. Like she's not got a worry in the world.

And I can't imagine Courtney lies awake at night with constant worries. She won't mind what she looks like, because she's confident enough. She won't fret that she doesn't know who she is. She won't worry that she doesn't truly know what she wants to do for a living, so she then ends up trying to do so many things—and failing.

I take out my phone and put it onto the front camera so my face fills the screen. I start recording. "And I've just finished writing Courtney in as the villain," I say, and I feel my excitement bubbling up. "Let me read you an excerpt."

I search for a good passage to read, and I'm nearly laughing as I see Courtney's name. "How about this one—this is a great bit. We see 'Courtney' being arrested, only for her then to break out of custody using a pair of shoelaces."

I read the section, using my best voice acting, and then film my laptop screen as I upload that draft to the various eBook platforms—I've still got a few days to replace the file, so I'll do that with the correct version as soon as the platform allows the upload of a new document. Probably tomorrow. I mean, the real file's ready to go anyway.

Once all is done, I send the clip to Zara via Dropbox. She replies with a solitary 'thanks' and nothing else. She doesn't even have an email signature. Wow.

Sergeant mews at me for more food, so I search through Victoria's cupboards. He finished the last box earlier, with the bowlful then, and I can't find where the spare boxes of cat food are kept.

"Sorry, Sergeant, you may have just have to wait until Victoria's back." I glance at the clock. Victoria is visiting her sister, and I don't think she'll be back for a while.

Sergeant's mews get louder and more pitiful. In the end, I end up cutting a hunk of cheese off the block and giving it to him. He purrs loudly, and I smile. Then I set about feeding all the other animals. For a small-ish apartment, there sure are a lot packed in here. Four budgies take up residence in the open-plan living space, in a massive cage, and the end part of the kitchen, just beyond the counter, is where Shelley the Tortoise lives. I smile as I look at Shelley. She was my dad's. Dad had got her when he was a little boy, and I grew up with Shelley too. After Dad died, Shelley went to live with Victoria. I mean, I was offered him, but Adam wouldn't have an animal in the house. Said they were all too unclean.

I cut up some kale and collard greens that I find in the fridge and then arrange them carefully in Shelley's vivarium. She is awake, eyeing the food, but doesn't move toward it. I shrug. I thought kale was her favorite.

After I've fed the budgies too, and the bearded dragon who's in a tank in Martin's room, I pull out my laptop again. I close the manuscript files and instead navigate toward my online business. The virtual shopper. But when I try to concentrate on it, I find myself thinking about Courtney. What prank is she planning now? I wonder when she's going to put her plan into place. Or maybe she already has—she could've done something similar to me, but I wouldn't necessarily know… not until I watch Zara's film, which she's promised we will. Then I guess I'll know just how much Courtney hates me.

SEVENTEEN

Courtney

"HELLO, THIS IS Places for Aces. You're speaking to Tabitha. How can I help?" I adjust my headset a little, so it's not pulling quite so much on my hair—somehow, I left the house earlier without brushing it, and only noticed just now as I arrived at the center when I caught my reflection in a darkened window.

"Hello," the caller says. A female voice, very timid. I'm relieved it's not Sophie—we're in the timeslot now that she called last week: Sunday evening. "Uh, I just… I think I'm ace, and I just… this is a bit weird."

"It's okay," I say. "Take your time. I'm just here to listen." I stretch my feet out.

"Well, I was just wondering about whether it's normal to be afraid of being naked. Like, not just around other people, but just when it's me too. I just, I can't stand it. And I'm with this guy—he's not ace—and I just keep thinking he's going to expect me to be naked around him, even if we don't have sex. Like, I mean, he's going to want to *see* me, especially if he can't do anything with me, because I don't want to have sex. And I just get really nervous now any time I see him."

"Okay," I say, keeping my voice smooth and calm. Gentle, as Mrs. Mitchell would say. "So, it's perfectly normal for people to not like being naked, whether they're around others or not. And that's normal for some people who are ace and some who are not. There's no definite rule for that, it's very much an individual thing. But, uh—do you mind telling me your name?"

There's a slight pause. "Carly."

"Well, Carly. You say that you think your boyfriend is going to expect to see you naked? Has he actually said this?"

"Well, no...but he tries to undress me."

"And have you told him you're not comfortable with that?"

"Well, sort of."

"Okay," I say. "Because it sounds like he's trying to cross a boundary with you, and it's perfectly okay if you're not comfortable with that—but you shouldn't feel pressured to do things that make you feel uncomfortable."

Her breathing gets a little louder. "I just feel that I'll *have* to be naked around him—like, he's not getting sex, so this is the compromise?"

"A compromise still needs to be something you're comfortable with, Carly. You know the feeling you get when something's wrong or making you feel on edge? Yeah? We have that for a reason. It's our gut trying to protect us—not always from obvious danger, but from doing things that we're not comfortable with."

"It's like, if I could say it was an ace thing—that none of us like being naked—I think he'd get it more than if I just say *I* don't like being naked. He respects me being ace. Like, I've never liked being without my clothes."

"So, you're worried that if he knows it's not part of being ace, that he won't respect your preference for no nudity?" I ask.

"Well, yeah—and that makes him sound like a dick, and I don't mean to convey him like that. Because he's not. But I'm just worried."

My chair creaks as I shift my weight. "I think you need to just talk to him," I say. "Communication is key in any relationship. And he should respect your wishes for no nudity. He shouldn't pressure you."

"It would just be easier if I could say it was part of being ace."

"It may well be that a dislike of nudity is part of *your* own identity as an asexual," I say, because I can tell that she really wants me to say that it is part of being ace—only it isn't, not for everyone. I know plenty of ace-spec people who are very comfortable with nudity, both being naked around others and having others naked around them.

She makes a *mmhmm* sound. "Well, uh, thanks."

"That's okay, Carly. Is there anything else you'd like to talk about?"

"No."

She hangs up rather abruptly—and I mean, a lot of callers do that, especially if they've got one specific question they want to ask or something they're worried about. I chew on my bottom lip. I hope what I said did help her.

"Oh my god, you're gonna win this, hands down," Zara mutters as she slides into the seat next to me. It's the next morning, and seeing as I don't work Mondays, and I've invited the twins round for brunch. "Sophie's prank is so lame."

"Lame isn't a PC word," I point out. "But what's the prank?"

"Can't tell you," Zara says. "But seriously, you're gonna have no problem winning this, hands down—like I said."

"Yeah, I expected more of Sophie," Zoe says. She glances at me—tentatively. All her glances have been like that since she knew that Zara told us about her diagnosis. Twice, I've tried to talk to her about it, but she just clams up every time. "I watched the footage she sent, and wow, it's like she's not even competitive any more. Weird."

"Well, people change," I say. But Sophie not being competitive *is* weird when I think of what she was like at school. How we were friendly rivals, until that day that ruined everything.

"Yeah," Zoe mutters. She stands up. "See you later."

"You're going already?" Zara asks.

Zoe nods, doesn't offer explanation, just leaves. We listen to the sound of the door bang, and then stare awkwardly at each other.

"She hates me," Zara says. "I'm sure she does. I mean, I'd hate me too, if I was her. God, I need to do something to make things up with her." She looks at me. "Any ideas?"

"Maybe we should do some research or something. Find a good doctor?" I suggest. There's time for us to do research now. The only thing I have planned is a shift at the center later. "I mean, surely if she knows that we're by her side in this, that'll help?"

Zara nods. "I hope you're right."

EIGHTEEN

Sophie

"HOW ARE THE pre-orders going?" Victoria asks me over a late breakfast. "For the new book?"

I bring the screen up on my phone and carefully spear one of my half-grapes with the prongs of my fork. Today is grapes and melon for breakfast, followed by kefir and oats. It's written in my meal planner. "Very well. Forty-one, so far."

Victoria clasps her hands together, looking genuinely delighted. "Your father always said you'd be famous."

"It's hardly famous," I mutter, and her words just make me feel awkward. It's ridiculous that she thinks this is famous—or even successful. But the truth is, I've got no idea what I'm doing, self-publishing. I just wanted to get my book out fast once I'd finished editing the manuscript. I need to be able to hold it in my hands, a tangible thing that proves I'm good—or okay—at something.

"Still, that reminds me," I say to Victoria, "I need to upload the final file of it, today or tomorrow though, before the upload function is locked tomorrow at midnight, as then it'll be too close to the release date."

"I'm just so proud of you." Victoria beams. "How wonderful to have an author in the family."

I nod and smile, yet I can't help but feel like a fraud.

Half the time, I feel like I'm just trying to be good at something now—because when I was a model, I felt good all the time. Then all that shit happened, and now it's just me and I'm reaching out for something that could, just maybe, be mine.

My ex completely burst my dreams of being an actor, what with his comments and remarks, so that feels out of reach now. Unattainable. But I never told him I wanted to be a writer— and really, it's something I only realized toward the end of our relationship. When he was gambling our lives away in the pub on the main street, I'd started drafting out a story.

When I first began writing it, it was more of a screenplay- type-thing. Something that I thought I could act in and play the main character. I constructed the whole story so that it evolved around the victim—me—as she was stalked by her ex. Originally, the ex had been male, but I'd ended up a little worried that my actual ex would somehow end up reading it and accuse me of writing shit about him—when of course it was all fictional. But Adam's one of those people who just thinks the world revolves around him.

I've known I was bi since I was a teenager, but Adam once said to me that he thought bi people just were 'ashamed to be gay and so used the bi label instead'—I mean, that should've been my first warning sign with him—and so I never told him I thought I was bi too. That's if I still can be counted as bi, what with being ace. And there I go—back to worrying about definitions and everything.

I sigh. My stomach rumbles, begs for food.

But I can't do it.

"Hello, this is Places for Aces," Tabitha says.

I recognize her voice immediately, and I cut her off before she has a chance to confirm that it actually is her. "Hi Tabitha, it's me again. Sophie. Um, I hope you don't mind me calling you. Again. I mean, you just happened to pick up again, so it was more me calling the helpline and…" I feel my face reddening. I'm rambling. Brilliant.

"Not at all," Tabitha says, and her voice is so smooth and lulling. "It's lovely to hear from you again, Sophie. How've you been?"

"Uh, good," I say, blinking hard. Suddenly, my mind goes blank, and I can't think of a single thing to say about my week. I mean, there's all the prank stuff and my book, but that just seems silly to say that now—I don't even know Tabitha. And she's not here to listen to general stuff.

"That's great to hear," Tabitha says, and I wonder if that's a line she's been prepped to say. I mean, she can't genuinely think it's *great*. "So, how can I help you today?" she asks. When I pause, she adds, "Is there anything in particular you'd like to talk about?"

I fidget a little. I'm perched on the edge of my bed, one leg crossed over the other, and my feet are already getting pins and needles. I mean, that happens a lot. Poor circulation and that. "Yes." I clear my throat. "Um, so I've been reading a lot about the definitions of all the different…" I fish for the right word.

"The different identities that come under the ace spectrum. And there are just so many, and I'm very confused, but I... I want to find the ones that most relate to me, if that makes sense?"

"Of course that makes sense," Tabitha says. "Some individuals find this very helpful in giving a sense of identity and belonging."

Belonging. All I've ever wanted.

I clear my throat again, then lower my voice. "I was particularly wondering about how asexuality works if you're attracted to men and women?" I look around quickly, heart pounding, almost expecting to see Victoria or Martin listening in, hiding in the corner of my room. But neither's here—of course not. "Like, I've read about biromanticism and bisexuality, but I'm just confused."

"In what way are you confused?"

"Well, I'm sort of accepting now that I am probably ace. But I've only had relationships with men—and I'm not sexually attracted to them. Like, just... I like kissing and hugging, and some touching so long as it's not...you know...down there. But I am attracted to women too—still not sexually, but more...like their appearance? I think they look more attractive to me, aesthetically. But I'm also drawn to women too, emotionally. And I'm just confused really. It's like I have sensual attraction to men, but emotional and aesthetic to women—yet I just..." I look down at my notebook where I've written this all out. I drew out a diagram last night of the different types of attraction as I tried to pinpoint where I was. "But then romantic attraction seems to be a big thing in the ace world, whether you have it or not, and I just... I can't work out if I'm biromantic, because I've only been romantically involved with men before. And then I don't know whether to call myself a biromantic ace or heteromantic ace." My voice is shrill, like it always is when I'm stressed. But I need to know this. I need to know what I am.

"Okay," Tabitha says. "Just take a deep breath, Sophie. Look, whether you're heteromantic or biromantic, it won't change whether you're ace or not."

"But I want to know what type I am."

"And it's valid to want to know that, I get that. Working out exactly which label best suits you can be so affirming—but it sounds like you're putting a lot of pressure on yourself, and labels aren't useful for everyone if it feels restrictive. Perhaps it would be better to take your time with this, Sophie? And, remember, that what one identifies as is a personal choice," Tabitha says. "No one can tell you you're wrong, if that's how you feel. The important thing to remember is that asexuality is a spectrum. It covers many different identities, and if choosing a more specific label is helpful for you, then you should do it, but that doesn't mean that you can't redefine how you identify later."

I frown. "What do you mean?"

"Well, I, for example, used to believe I was demi-sexual—and maybe I *was* then. But right now, I describe myself as ace, rather than demi, as I feel it better represents me. So that's what I use."

"Okay," I say. "I guess I'm just worried. Like, if I choose the wrong label now and tell some people, then I change my mind later and realize something else suits better? How am I going to get people to believe me if I just look like I'm changing my mind? Like I don't even know what I'm talking about?"

There's a slight clicking noise, and then I hear background noise where Tabitha is. A woman's voice. But Tabitha continues, "So, are you worried people aren't going to believe you? Is that why you're stressed about choosing the right term now?"

I shrug. "Maybe. I—I don't know."

"If you don't mind me asking, who are you thinking of telling?"

I clutch the phone tighter. "My step-mother. Maybe my step-brother too. They're the only family I've got now. And I just feel like I should tell them. Like they deserve to know the truth."

"Well, that has to be your decision, and I suggest only doing so if you're comfortable. But remember, in telling anyone about your identity, if they're not aware of the ace spectrum, the important thing is to emphasize that it's exactly that—a spectrum. And it's important that you also realize that you can change where you sit on the spectrum at any point, if a new place seems more fitting for you."

I nod, and thank Tabitha before we end the call. She's right—I know that. But I can't help this burning desire I have to find out exactly what type of asexual I am—as, if I can reach out and grab that word now, close it in my fist and hold it close, then no one can take it away from me. I'll have something that's really my own, something that tells me who I am. And that will be calming, reassuring. And I need that. Because, right now, thinking about telling Victoria, my bottom lip is trembling.

Stop being silly, I tell myself. *It'll be fine.*

But I'm scared about how she'll react. She tries to be liberal and understand people in the LGBT community—and she is a lot more accepting of it now. But I also know how she reacted shortly after she married my father, when they moved into a cottage and the neighbors were a lesbian couple. She never said anything bad to them, but I could tell what she was thinking by the things she said to us. Nothing outright homophobic or anything, but she treated those neighbors differently to the others on the lane. And I just don't know how she'll react if I reveal I'm ace. Or biromantic ace or whatever.

I end up worrying myself silly about it all through the night and the next day too. My body's still jittery with nerves by the time I go to bed on Tuesday, and I feel lightheaded. Talking to Tabitha yesterday about the possibility of being biromantic has just made it seem all the more real, and I had a job to appear normal at dinner with Victoria earlier. Martin was out at football practice, so it was just the two of us. And the air felt strangely charged.

"You all right?" she'd asked me as I cut up my carefully-sized portion of quiche into six triangles.

I'd nodded, even though I felt sick and the smell of the quiche wasn't helping.

Now, my empty stomach churns and churns, and I curl onto my side, wrapping my duvet around me tighter.

It will be okay, won't it?

I wake in a cold sweat, heart pounding, my head spinning with dreams of Victoria throwing me out, and Martin laughing, and me holding my book in my hands, and Victoria snatching it from me and throwing it in a lake that just materializes behind her when she needs to get rid of the book because she says the main relationship in the book isn't as God intended.

And I don't know why I dreamt of that, when Victoria's never said those words. She's not even religious. And she wouldn't throw my book away, I'm sure, because—

My book.

My eyes widen.

The draft.

No.

I bolt upright and look at my clock. It's *Tuesday.* For a second, I freeze, as if by doing so I can freeze time as well. But the neon numbers blink 11.58. I have two minutes until the file uploaded for pre-order is locked.

Two minutes.

"Shit, shit, shit," I mutter, springing out of bed. I knock stationary from my desk as I grab my laptop and turn it on. "Come on!" I stare at the loading icon.

The neon numbers on my alarm clock flick to 11.59.

Oh God. Oh God. Oh God.

And, of course, this makes me shaky. I mistype my password several times, and I'm nearly crying. This can't be happening—this—

I let out a small gasp as my bedside clock changes to 00:00. "No… no!"

Fervently, I hope that my clock is fast—only I know it's always right. But still, I log onto my laptop, getting the password right this time, and then bring up the browser and log into the self-publishing platform.

My heart sinks as I see the message. *This pre-order is locked. Changes can't be made.*

I let out a shaky breath.

Oh God. My book is going to be published with Courtney as the villain.

NINETEEN

Sophie

"YES, YES, YES!" Zara yells in my ear, her face up close to me. "This is exactly the drama I need!"

She shoves her phone at me, and I try to wave her away as I recoil back. "Can you stop?" I hiss, still trying to listen to the ringing tone on my phone. My hands are sweating so much and twice already I've nearly dropped my mobile.

"Put it on speaker," Zara hisses.

"You're not filming this!"

"Of course I am," Zara says. "This is authentic drama. This can't be scripted. Now, put the damn phone on speaker."

When I don't make a move to do so, she reaches past me and does it—just as my call is answered.

"Hello, you're through to Janey Cogswell-Walker at—"

"Is that Janey?" Zara's eyes are wide.

I nod and try to turn my back on Zara, but of course she dances around me. "Janey, hi. It's Sophie. Sophie Sway. Look, I need your help."

In a stage whisper, Zara says, "For viewers who don't know, Janey Cogswell-Walker, formerly known as Janey Cogswell, is the—"

"Can you be quiet?" I hiss at Zara. I don't even want her here. All night, I tossed and turned as I replayed the actions that led to my error. I eventually decided the best course of action was to contact Janey. We may not have spoken in years, but she's a lawyer now. Apparently, a very successful one too.

But just as I was about to phone her, Zara turned up with her camera, demanding to know how the game was going. Given how little sleep I've had, I'd ended up crying and explaining it to her in gulps, before I continued trying to call Janey.

"Sorry, Janey—things are a bit chaotic here," I say, shooting a glare Zara's way.

"So, what's the problem?" Janey asks. Her voice is poised and stern. She sounds like she's middle-aged, not mid-twenties.

In gulps, I explain what's happened, trying to pretend that Zara isn't filming the whole thing and looking delighted.

"Can I get sued for this?" I grip my phone tighter, spitting out the question the moment I've finished telling the story.

Zara's eyes are huge circles as she stares at me. She couldn't look happier if she tried.

"Well, in theory. I mean, you've made her identifiable using her real name, description, and the town she lives in." Janey sighs. "I mean, Sophie, what the hell were you thinking?"

"It was for a prank show."

"A prank show?" Janey asks.

"*My* prank show," Zara says, looking proud as punch.

"Look, the prank show doesn't matter," I say. "It's still done—and I don't know what to do. I mean, there's only forty pre-orders or something. It'll be fine, right, Janey? And once it's midnight on release day, I can change the file."

I take deep breaths, and I wait for Janey to tell me of course it will be fine. Or to say that she'll represent me if it's not. That she'll do everything to make sure I don't get in trouble. Because I can't go to prison—I mean, could I even go to prison for this? I take deep breaths.

"I think you need to tell Courtney what has happened," Janey says. "She may be okay with it. In which case, you'll be fine. I think that's your first step."

I feel sick as we end the call, and Zara's fluttering around me. "We've got to get the lighting in here sorted. Can I open the curtain more?"

"What?"

She rolls her eyes. "Sophie, we're about to film a massive scene for the project—You're going to invite Courtney round now and reveal this secret. Oh God, this is going to be amazing. Wait, where are you going?"

I'm halfway to the door when I stop. "To tell her at her house. Zara, can you just stop all this. This is serious. This isn't a prank any more—this could really hurt her."

A sly look crosses into her eyes. "Oh, so you're worried about hurting her now? Wow."

I ignore her and head out. Of course she follows me with the camera still running.

My heart pounds as I head down the stairs.

When I knock on Courtney's door, I'm shaking, actually shaking. My legs have never felt so weak. I've felt so weak.

She doesn't answer, and I look at Zara.

"Well, she'll be at work."

"At work?" I run a hand through my hair. I've got to wait a whole day to see Courtney, to try and sort this horrible mess out.

"It's only in Exeter," Zara says. "Let's go. We could get there when she's having a break."

An hour later, we're outside Courtney's office.

"She's coming now," Zara says. She has just texted Courtney.

I count the seconds until the door opens, and Courtney appears. Her hair's a mess and she looks surprised to see us. Surprised and cute and—

No.

I take a deep breath. "I'm so sorry," I say.

"What?" Courtney looks from me to Zara. "Bloody hell, Zara, you could've warned me we were filming today. And at my work, too? John's not going to be happy."

"Spur of the moment thing," Zara says, then she nudges me. Actually nudges me.

I glare at her, only for a second though, then turn to Zara. "I am so sorry. This… My prank's gone wrong."

"What prank?" Courtney frowns, and it just makes her look all the more innocent. A confused baby deer or something.

"The book one," I say. "Where you're the villain." I take a deep breath and pour out the whole story before I can chicken out.

Zara makes dramatic noises which would've made me snap at her if I wasn't so worried about Courtney's reaction. Courtney whose life I could've just ruined…because what if some reader thinks it's real and comes around here to get revenge on Courtney? To kill her, just as she kills the main character in my book at the end?

Oh God. I'm going to have to guard Courtney. Be her bodyguard or something and—

Courtney laughs. Actually laughs.

I take a small step back, but she's still laughing.

"Wow. I'm going to be famous," she says.

I shake my head. "No, you're not getting the seriousness of this—you're the *villain*. You're a stalker in this. It's about this stalker going after her ex-girlfriend."

"It's a Sapphic story?" Courtney's eyebrows shoot up.

"Yeah," I say. "But look, I'm so sorry. And I can change it once it's release day. I have the real file ready to just swap with it. But forty-ish people are going to get this version. I can't seem to stop that."

"So, I will be famous?" Courtney asks. "Famous to forty-ish people. Wow. Who would've thought that you of all people would make me famous?"

I groan. "Look, I'm so sorry. Uh, please don't sue me."

"Sue you?" Courtney frowns.

"Nah, wait," Zara says. "You should leave that version up— if it's okay with Court. I mean, this is juicy drama. And my project gets broadcast in a few months. It could really amp up your book sales, Sophie."

I stare at her. Since when has Zara ever been concerned about helping me?

"You could have a sticker on the front of it or something that says 'as seen on Queen of Pranks,'" Zara says.

Courtney's blinking slowly, a slight frown on her face as she stares at Zara too. Is she thinking the same thing?

I swallow hard. The roof of my mouth is dry. Too dry. Like I've recovered it with sandpaper.

"So it's really okay?" I ask Courtney. "You're not going to sue me?"

She shakes her head. "Nah, I just need to think of an even better prank to get you back with."

TWENTY

Courtney

LATE AFTERNOON, BACK at my apartment, I have no idea what prank to do next on Sophie, so of course I turn to Google—Zara didn't say anything about us having to come up with the prank ideas ourselves. I try to find another ghostly prank, but apart from dressing myself in a white sheet with eye-holes, just like in cartoons, I can't find anything that I could actually do. So, instead, I scroll through pages and pages of suggestions for 'ultimate pranks' and 'pranks to play on friends'—though Sophie is most definitely not a friend—until I find one that I like. It's a good one too.

I give Zara a ring and tell her of my idea.

She approves of it but doesn't seem as enthusiastic as she did for the ghost stuff. Still, I guess Sophie's mistake is going to be the highlight of the film. Zara said earlier she might even restructure it all in edits so it looks like that is the climax of the whole game.

"You'll have to get Mrs. Dalton to approve of this too," Zara says, before we end the call.

I head over to the Daltons' quickly. Sophie already told Zara and I that she was going out this evening, when they caught me earlier at the office—she has some Pilates class or something that she was joining—and so I think it will just be Mrs. Dalton home at this time. It's almost six o'clock, and she smiles widely when she sees me.

"Come in, come in," she says, and I wonder if she knows about Sophie's mistake with the book. If she does, she doesn't say anything about it. She just chats away, asking me about how my work's going, how my mum is, and how lovely it is that Sophie and I have made up. I'm not entirely sure where she's got that last idea from, but I don't correct her.

Then I move onto the reason for my visit: quickly, I explain my idea, and to my surprise, she's up for it. Maybe she thought it would be a more dangerous prank or something? But this isn't at all really. Just on the annoyance level.

"Oh wow," Mrs. Dalton says, once I've explained everything and when I want to carry it out.

"Think you can help me with this?" I ask.

She nods. "Of course. You just leave it to me. You'd better get back to your apartment—Fifi will be back home soon."

"But the eggs," I say.

She taps the side of her nose. "I'll do them tonight, once Fifi's gone out for her run." She claps her hands together. "Gosh, isn't this going to be fun?"

Back in my apartment, I turn my attention to Google and read up more on endometriosis. I make a list of private doctors that

I can find who are specialists—and read way more about gynecologists' fields of interest than I ever want to—and then set about finding reviews for these doctors.

I put all the info into a spreadsheet, and then email it over to Zara. Then, I call Zoe. I don't expect her to answer, because she rarely does, but when the line clicks and she says, "Hello," I scramble for something to say.

"Uh, how are you?" I ask.

She sighs a long sigh that translates beautifully down the phone. "You don't need to constantly be worrying about me now. Nothing's actually changed in terms of symptoms. You didn't care that much before—before you knew it was real."

"I'm so sorry," I say.

She makes a sound in her throat—maybe her clearing it, I'm not sure. "Well, I suppose it was more my sister doing that than you."

I take a deep breath. "Look, if you want to talk about it, then I'm here. But, equally, if you'd rather not talk about it, then I'm also here—like whatever you need from me, I'm here."

"Thanks." I have a feeling she's saying it with a tight-lipped smile. "But I've got to go. Got a migraine."

"Oh, sorry. Hope you feel better." I wince at how fake that sounds. God, I'm awful at this. No wonder she didn't say anything.

Zoe says goodbye and my head spins as I sit down.

I need to be a better friend—that much is clear. Things shouldn't be like this between us.

I'll do better, I silently promise her.

TWENTY-ONE

Sophie

IT'S OMELET DAY. I follow a strict meal plan for the days of the week and Thursday is Omelet For Lunch Day.

Victoria's sitting at the table, her phone in her hand. She's frowning intently at something.

I grab two eggs from the fridge and go to crack the first on the edge of the frying pan and—

It's hard boiled. What the hell?

I frown. I try the other. It's the same.

I frown more and peel the two eggs and set them in a bowl in the fridge.

Only the next eggs I grab are *also* hard boiled.

Victoria stifles a giggle. She's standing right behind me, phone still in her hands.

"This is Courtney's prank?" I raise my eyebrows, irritation burning through me.

"Yes," Victoria laughs.

"Seriously, she came in here and hard boiled all my eggs because she knows I have omelets on Thursdays?"

Victoria nods, and I clock the phone in her hand.

"And you're filming this?"

"Yes. Courtney asked me to. She explained it all, and I think you two taking part in this game show is a great way to sort out your differences."

"Wow." I don't know what to say other than that. Just wow. I mean, seriously, hard-boiling all the eggs? That's a bit... well, not exciting. I expected better from her. She is my rival, after all.

Victoria sets the phone down on the counter. "Oh, I've been meaning to tell you," she says, moving toward me. She sits at the little table. "I've been helping a prince from Valinor. Awfully nice he is, and he's looking for a wife. I wondered if you'd be interested?"

"*What?*" I nearly choke.

"I know it's a bit of a shock." She smiles. "But he's really quite charming."

"No... wait—he's a prince from..." I'm breathing too quickly.

"Very good manners for a prince, I must say," Victoria says before I can even form more words. "You see, I got this email a few weeks ago, and he sounded like such a lovely man. He'd just had a lot of bad luck, and he needed a friend—I don't know how he found me, but I was happy to help. I mean, you know what it's like to need a friend, right?"

"This is..." My eyes are so wide they feel like they're going to pop. "How much have you given him?"

"It's just a loan, so you don't need to worry," she says.

"How much?"

"Fourteen thousand—but he's going to pay it back, and more, now that I've helped him get back on his feet."

I feel sick as I stare at her. "What the hell? Why... Martin—does he know? Why the hell didn't he stop you?"

She laughs and pushes her hair back from her face. "Oh, he doesn't know. I didn't want to worry him. You know what he's like. He's always thinking everything is a scam." She stands up and reaches for her phone, presses a button. "Let me show you his photo."

My chest feels too tight. "No, Victoria, this is a scam. Why would a prince from another country actually contact you?" I take a deep breath. "We have to report this to the police. We—"

"It's fine. It's not a scam." She rolls her eyes. "You sound just like Martin. You—"

There's a knock at the door—it makes me jump.

Victoria looks at me. "Can you get that?"

Heart pounding, with numb sensations filling me, I move to the door. My fingers are like ice. What if it's him? Not Victoria's scammer, but Adam? What if he barges his way in and hurts me? Hurts us?

I pull open the door.

"Surprise!" Courtney practically bursts through the doorway.

I jump back.

And—and what the hell is she wearing? A red velvet waistcoat, a green cloak, knee-length brown shorts?

"Get it?" She grins widely, and then reaches past me and high-fives Victoria who's suddenly right behind me.

I stare at them both.

"I'm the prince," Courtney says, laughing.

"Wait. Valinor?" I look at Victoria. "That's from *The Lord of the Rings*. And you..." I look at Courtney. "You're dressed as..."

"Frodo." She rolls her eyes.

I turn to Victoria again. "So, you haven't given away fourteen grand?"

She snorts. "Of course not. It was all a joke."

A joke. A prank.

"And I have to say, it was so much fun getting involved," Victoria says.

My heart is still hammering away. "You nearly gave me a heart attack."

"That was the plan," Courtney says, smiling. "Ha, your face!" She reaches round to the side of the hall, where the bookcase is, and she plucks something toward her. A small digital camera. "Though I honestly thought I wasn't going to get back from work in time—half day and that."

I frown and look at Victoria. "I thought you were filming it on your phone? And I thought it was the eggs?"

"That was to throw you off." She laughs, and then Courtney's laughing too.

I just smile. I'm not laughing. But seeing the way they do, how they laugh and laugh together, it just makes me feel like even more of an outside.

TWENTY-TWO

Sophie

"YOUR MOTHER'S SO proud of you." Dad gives me a sympathetic look as he stops the car at the athletics arena. "Whether you win or not, we're both proud of you."

I give a small smile, but I don't like it when he says 'we' now or how he still talks as if my mother's still alive. There's something about it that makes my skin crawl, but I can never say anything to him about it—not when the only time his eyes light up now is when he's talking like this, as if she's still alive.

"Thanks." I climb out of his Aston Martin. It's brand new and still has the new-car smell.

The rest of the athletics club is already here. They all took St. Bridget's mini bus, but Dad insisted on picking me up from school and driving me separately. I can't help but wonder what the other girls thought about that. Out of me and my friends, I'm the only sporty one—well, I try to take part in everything, just as my parents encouraged me—but it means that on St. Bridget's mini bus there'd have been no one there to speak up for me if one or two of the girls made unkind remarks, like saying I think I'm too good to use their transport.

I'm probably just over-reacting, but I can't help worrying they've been talking about me.

"I'll be in the stands," Dad says. He gives me a quick squeeze of the shoulder before he retreats to the usual stand—the one where he always sat with Mum, watching my performances.

"Okay." My voice has never been so small, and suddenly, I want to reach out, tell my dad to stay here with me. I don't want to be on my own.

But of course I can't do that. I just watch him go.

My eyes cross to the three nearest girls. Courtney and Zoe are stretching, while Zara's intently staring at her phone, typing away. Courtney's still not speaking to me, but I'm hoping today's going to change things. Traditionally, the fight for first place in the Pentathlon has always been between me and Courtney. She won in Year Ten, I won in Years Nine and Eight, and she again in Year Seven. This year's pentathlon almost feels like a tie-break. Me or her.

But whereas in other years when Courtney and I would chat and warm up together, she's now watching me, coldly. Her eyes are narrowed, and she says something to Zoe in a voice too low for me to hear.

I turn away, feeling goosebumps shiver up my arms. I scan the other girls, but everyone's in little groups now, chatting and laughing and warming up. With friends.

I wrap my arms around myself and breathe deeply. Try to think of my warm-up exercises as Ms. Palmer, the P.E. teacher, calls for us all to listen. She explains the usual rules—how we must be on our best behavior because we're representing the school—and then lets us know the schedule. We're here early, before the other schools, and it gives us a chance to breathe a bit first. Ms. Palmer promises that it makes a big difference.

"You don't want to be like the other girls competing," she says. "Arriving here five minutes before, frazzled, no time to warm up properly and acclimatize to your environment."

I just wish we'd get on with it, get this over with, so I can return back to the school. So, I can find my friends and feel less alone. But I know my dad will take me out for dinner. He always does.

The next hour goes by agonizingly slow. The other schools' teams arrive, and then the athletics arena is buzzing as it fills up with spectators.

"Right, Courtney Davenport and Sophie Sway, you're both representing us on the pentathlon," Ms. Palmer says.

I nod.

Courtney nods.

She doesn't look at me though. She just almost acts as if I'm not here, as we warm up for the shot put first.

It's even the same when we're competing—she doesn't look at me at all.

Courtney wins the 800 meters and the shot put. I win the long jump and the high jump. We check the leaderboard. I'm standing slightly behind Courtney, but she doesn't acknowledge me at all. I've got two more points than her, but the two of us are in the top two positions. Five points separate her from the next competitor.

"Just the hurdles to go," I say, and my voice wavers with nerves because I need her to acknowledge me.

She doesn't. I may as well be invisible.

"I think congratulations are in order." Dad's voice is warm but quiet as he leans in close to me at the restaurant. We're at an Italian place, and my stomach's churning away at the thought of how many calories are in the pizza I ordered.

"I don't want to make a big thing of it," I say, trying to give Dad a look that he'll know means business. I hunker down in my seat a little.

"But we're just so proud of you."

We. *There it is again. I wince.*

Dad reaches across the table and takes my hand. "I've never felt so proud," *he says, and there are tears in his eyes.* "You're really giving our name meaning. The Sways—people will know we're important when they see your name in the paper again."

I nod, weakly, but I can't help thinking of the look of disappointment I saw on Courtney's face. There was less than an eighth of a second between our finishes of the hurdles. It was a photo-finish and for several minutes afterward, we didn't know who had won.

But then when the plasma screen on the stadium updated to show that I had just edged the victory, I'd seen the way Courtney's face had dropped.

When I was called up onto the stage to get the gold medal, I'd been looking at her face. I was sure she was trying not to cry when she was called up for the silver.

The gold medal is still around my neck, and it feels bad, like it's weighing me down. And I don't know why I feel so bad about this, when I won the medal fair and square. I didn't do anything to sabotage her—so why does it feel like I did?

"Now, I've been talking to the Roakes," *Dad says, and I jerk back to the present.*

"The Roakes?"

He nods. "I think it would be a good idea if you met their son. You know, Bradley?"

"Bradley?" *I frown.*

"He's a very nice young man, and you're a beautiful girl."

My eyes narrow. "You're not suggesting…"

"It would be very beneficial to us," *he says.*

Beneficial? To us? A bitter taste spreads across the roof of my mouth.

"I've arranged for you two to meet, properly, next week," *he says.*

"Next week?"

"His father wants him married before he gets deployed."

"Married?" My heart races faster and faster. "No, Dad—"

"Just see what you think," he says, giving me a small smile. "Your mother thinks it's a great idea." That hopeful, almost dreamy look, returns to his eyes, and he smiles into the distance.

My stomach churns and churns. Half the time, I don't think he's accepted that my mother's gone. Really gone. Instead, he's just living in this fantasy land.

TWENTY-THREE

Courtney

SOPHIE IS NOT moving out, that much is clear—and maybe this prank competition has something to do with it. I could kick myself now for agreeing to this. But that's not the only bad thing. Sophie's also wanting to make the chat on the helpline a regular thing—in the last few days, since the prince-scam prank, she's called each evening. That's not unusual at all. Many callers do that. A couple years ago, we had some bloke called Harry phone us because he was in love with a girl he'd been to school with and he'd just found out she was asexual. He was desperate to know as much as possible, but didn't want to put the onus on the girl to become a teacher. He recognized that it wasn't her job to educate him, so he phoned us. I spoke to him weekly for two months.

And normally I don't mind regular callers. They almost feel like friends. Friends who I'd never actually meet or know in real life. And I like that distance, I do.

But Sophie is not someone I can compartmentalize like I did with Harry. We went to school together. We were rivals. And now she lives next door. We're neighbors, in a fierce competition, and it's a game. It's nothing like how it ended up being at school.

I have to tell her. I know that. I'm not the right listener for her—she'd be horrified if she knew it was me.

So, I promise myself that I will tell her who 'Tabitha' really is the next time she calls. I mean, it's not like that'll be breaking any rules, will it? I'm revealing information about myself, not one of the callers. So that'll be fine.

On Monday, I finish up at the office early and head straight to the center.

The phone rings the moment I sit down, and my eyes widen. How does she do it? How does Sophie know to call the moment I'm here?

I take a deep breath, lick my dry lips, and answer the phone. "Hello, this is Tabitha speaking at Places for Aces. How can I help you?"

I nearly wince, waiting to hear her voice.

"Hello, there."

It's not her. Some haughty-sounding woman instead.

"Hi," I say. "How can I help you?" I repeat, when there's silence.

"Right, well," the woman says. "My daughter just told me she's asexual, and I know that some people are, but I also know she isn't." In the background I can hear children playing. "I'm worried because she's just latching onto this, to be cool. It's not who she is. She's already got a son, so she's clearly not asexual, but she's telling people she is?"

"Okay, firstly I understand that it must have been a surprise, your daughter telling you this." I trace my pen over the Places for Aces logo on the leaflet in front of me, then dig a bit hard and the ink goes through onto the desk. I wipe it with my sleeve. "But I feel it's also important to let you know that whether she's got children or not, it has no bearing on whether she's asexual."

"But she's had sex!" The woman actually sounds scandalized.

I'm glad this isn't a video call because I can't help but roll my eyes. "And many asexual people do have sex. We're not asexual because of an inability or refusal to have sex. Asexual just means that you don't experience sexual attraction—some ace people have sex, some don't. It's not something that can be used to determine whether someone is ace or not."

The woman argues with me—just as I knew she would. We get a lot of callers like this.

And this call is followed by four more, all from similar types of people. I mean, I know I shouldn't really group people together like this, but we do get a lot of parents phoning up with similar arguments.

Sophie does not phone though, and I don't know whether I'm relieved to not have to tell her yet or annoyed that this whole thing is going to drag out more. I mean, why wasn't I honest upfront, as soon as I realized? And I've had plenty of opportunities in the last two weeks.

An hour later, when I leave the center and walk home in the icy dark, I'm still worrying about it, and I don't know why exactly I am. I mean, Sophie's reaction shouldn't be important to me at all.

I enter the Hawklands building, still trying to work out how Sophie will react. Is she going to be angry?

Outside my door, there's a parcel. A medium-sized box. A glance at the label tells me it's for Sophie.

I frown and look around for cameras or Zara giggling somewhere, semi-hidden. Is this the next prank? I listen, but it's quiet.

I take another look at the box. Nothing to say that it is a prank. Maybe it just got delivered to the wrong door? Though it shouldn't have been left out here.

I yawn as I hoist the box up into my arms. It's heavy, but I reason that taking it to Sophie's door is the neighborly thing to do. Humming, I take the stairs, and a few minutes later, I'm in the corridor on the floor above.

That's when I see the Daltons' door is open. Only a foot or so, but definitely open. I roll my eyes. No wonder dear Sergeant Ginger Paws is always escaping. Hell, I bet he's not even in there now.

Or maybe this is part of the prank set-up?

"Hello?" I call out.

Only silence meets me. I frown and push the door open a little.

I gasp as I see the wreckage. Tables and chairs on their sides, and a filing cabinet has been upturned.

I drop the parcel, and rush from room to room, suddenly expecting to see all manners of horrible things. Mrs. Dalton and Sophie and Martin all lying somewhere, covered in blood? But, no, there's no one here. Just the wreckage.

I inhale sharply as I see Mrs. Dalton's teacup collection—it's in hundreds of tiny pieces on the floor.

I call the police—this *can't* be a prank—and they arrive thirty-five minutes later when I'm sitting just outside the door, the cat in my lap. He was still in there, as were the budgies—including Arthur, the infamous escapee—but the tortoise and bearded dragon have gone. My phone's on the carpet next to me.

"I've tried calling Mrs. Dalton," I tell the officer as he writes down details. "But she didn't pick up."

"And you don't know what's been stolen?" he asks.

I shake my head. "No, not other than the tortoise and the bearded dragon. Well, I assume it's been stolen. I know they have one and there's an empty vivarium in there."

After telling me in a gruff voice that I shouldn't have gone in and disrupted a crime scene, the officer allows me to go back to my apartment. Sergeant Ginger Paws follows me, walks straight into my apartment like he owns the place.

I let out a sigh, but it's mainly for dramatic effect, because I reach down and affectionately tickle him behind the ears. He purrs.

"I guess we'd better just wait," I tell him, and I'm glad he's here, that I won't be waiting alone because suddenly I can't get rid of all these scenarios that are filling my head—Sophie and her family being drugged and dragged out of the house. Sophie and her family being held at gunpoint. Sophie and her family—

I cut that thought off. Got to stay calm.

But it frightens me. It frightens me a lot, and as I go back to pick up the parcel I dropped, I can't help but worry.

Two hours later, Mrs. Dalton returns my calls. She, Sophie, and Martin have been visiting her parents and are staying overnight there in Dorset. I break the bad news.

Another two hours and the trio are back, cutting short their visit. Sophie's shaking and her eyes are red. She stands behind her step-mother, still visibly trembling. Martin has the bearded dragon in a cat-carrier.

Mrs. Dalton and Martin just look annoyed. But Sophie seems distraught—this is not the Sophie I knew from school. This is a different person.

"I'm not sure if anything was taken apart from the tortoise," I say. "But the police have been inside, taking photos."

"Right. The tortoise passed away last night," Mrs. Dalton says.

"Oh," I say, and I feel like I've lost my footing or something. "Well, uh, the police say you can't stay there as forensics are going in, in the morning. But you can stay at mine. I've got blankets and stuff."

"Thank you, dear," Mrs. Dalton says.

"It's *him*," Sophie says, turning to Mrs. Dalton. "I told you it was him—he's... Is he still round here?" She looks at me. "Did you see him?"

"Who?" I blink.

"My ex. Adam. He's about this high." She holds a hand up to her eye-level. "White, blond hair, medium-sized build. Was he here?"

"I didn't see anyone," I say, but my chest tightens. Sophie's scared—that much is clear. Is this ex of hers dangerous?

"Don't worry," Mrs. Dalton says, enclosing Sophie's hand with her own. "It will be okay."

"But he's after me—the texts proved it!"

"The texts?" I say.

Mrs. Dalton looks harried. "He's all talk, Fifi," she says. "That's all. This is just a coincidence."

"Or it's a warning," Sophie mutters.

TWENTY-FOUR

Courtney

IT SEEMS MEAN to play any pranks on Sophie when she's staying at mine—and so obviously distraught about an ex coming after her—so I concentrate on being the welcoming host as I gather blankets and spare pillows. I've got a double bed and I make that up for Mrs. Dalton and Sophie. Martin says he'll stay with a friend—in fact, he seems eager to get away—which leaves me to have the sofa.

Sophie mumbles a thank-you before disappearing into my room. She's barely said anything since moving into mine—even earlier, when they were making a list of all their belongings and things of value in their apartment, to give to the police, she was so quiet. That outburst she had about her ex seemed to have used all her energy.

I look at Mrs. Dalton. "Is she okay?" I ask, as Sergeant Ginger Paws rubs against my legs.

She nods. "She and Adam just had a very messy breakup," she says. "He sent some texts before, saying that he'd find her—but we didn't think anything of it. And now she's convinced he's been here, done this to make a point."

I let out a long breath. "You told the police this?"

Mrs. Dalton nods. "They said they'd look into it. Of course, it could just be a coincidence. But I guess we'll find out. See what kind of stuff's been taken."

I nod. The police took their lists and said they'd correlate it with what's in the apartment. Most of the things I saw in there looked broken, but I didn't notice anything out of the ordinary being missing. The TV was still there—albeit the screen smashed.

Hell, everything was smashed. Must've made one hell of a racket. I wonder who was home at that time, which of the neighbors may have heard anything. Why didn't anyone call the police then?

"Anyway, thank you, dear," Mrs. Dalton says. "I'd best get some sleep. It's been a long day."

I find out the next morning what was stolen. One laptop— Sophie's. The police have just called. Sophie and I are the only ones up. Mrs. Dalton is still sleeping, and I've called work to let them know I'm going to be late. John was quite understanding and said I could probably just work from home later today to catch up.

"I knew the moment we heard that it was him," she says, sniffing. "And my laptop. God, just thinking about him going through my stuff, it's so violating. And he always said he'd pawn my laptop. Said it was his."

"What?"

"Because he bought it for me, before he got this gambling problem." She shakes her head. "I've got so much important stuff on there."

"You haven't got copies?" I ask.

"Oh my god. You sound like my dad. He was always saying that." Her face tightens—and I don't know if it's the mention of her late father that does it or not. I haven't heard her speak about her father once since she came here, yet at St. Bridget's, Sophie was always mentioning him. *My father works at…*. and *Just wait until I tell my father this.*

"I take that as a no then," I say, stepping back.

"I'm sorry," Sophie says. "I was mean yesterday. I know you stopped the cat from escaping permanently, and it wasn't your fault we were robbed. Look uh, do you have any coffee?"

"Sorry. I've run out of it."

She looks close to tears.

"I can go and get some?" I offer.

"Let's both go," she says. "I just want to get out of this whole building for a bit. We can get coffee at that shop on the corner. You know, the one with the tartan theme?"

"You want to get coffee…with me?"

She rolls her eyes. "Well, yeah."

And with that, she's off.

The coffee shop is loud and bustling.

"This is weird," I say, eventually voicing the one thought that's been spinning through my head, ever since I left a note for Mrs. Dalton, locked my door, and hurried to catch up with Sophie.

"Weird?" she asks, tilting her head to one side.

"Well, yeah." I gesture between us at the coffee table, and how we're sitting here, talking—like we're good friends. "Like, especially given we weren't friends at school."

She looks down at the table and focuses on stirring her coffee with the spoon. I went for hot chocolate, and it's too bitter for my liking, but I can't see any sugar sachets about.

"Are you still in contact with anyone from St. Bridget's?" Sophie asks after a moment, just as I'm contemplating whether to ask her about Adam. I can't deny that I'm curious—but I'm also worried too.

I shift in my seat. "Other than the twins, whom I'm related to, not really. I mean, there were a lot of brats at that school."

I see the look of hurt flash across her face. I don't apologize though—because she did hurt me. And even if it was Janey that did that PowerPoint slide, Sophie didn't have to go back to being friends with her.

"Fair," she says after a long minute.

"Are you?" I ask.

She shakes her head. "Well, most contact I've had was phoning Janey the other day when I was worried you were going to sue me." She laughs. "She's a lawyer now. But yeah…haven't spoken to her in years. I mean, I tried to keep in touch with some of the girls. Rebecca and Stacey, you know? But I don't know. It felt like I grew up, and they didn't. I met up with Stacey a year ago, and she was just… I don't know how to describe it really. We were in this pub, and she was just judging everyone in there. Like not even subtly. We saw one woman with four kids and yeah, maybe they shouldn't be in a pub, but Stacey was just badmouthing the mum. Saying she was a single mother obviously, that all the kids had different dads and the woman was spending her child benefit on getting drunk. The woman gave us such a stink eye, like Stacey was speaking so loudly, but yeah, Stacey was saying stuff like that about everyone. It just made me realize she wasn't a nice person. Even five minutes into seeing her, I knew there was no way I could be friends with her again. And that was Stacey of all people. She was always the most mellow out of our group."

I nod. "Makes sense. I mean, looking back at it now, pretty much all the girls at St. Bridget's were like that." *Including you.* But, of course, I don't say those last two words. Something stops me. I don't want to upset her more than she already is.

"I'm sorry," she says suddenly. "The way I treated you at school wasn't right. I was a brat."

I laugh. "Yeah. You were."

And I expect her to laugh too—only she doesn't.

"Do people give you a hard time still?" she asks.

"A hard time? What do you mean?"

Her brows furrow. "About being..." She lowers her voice. "Asexual. I mean—you are still asexual, right? I've never seen a boyfriend at your place or anything."

My eyes narrow. She's been watching my place? She's only been here just over two weeks! "Ace people can have relationships though," I say. "Seeing a guy at mine wouldn't mean I'm not. Because I am—still ace, that is."

And I wait for her to say it too—wait and wait. But she doesn't. She just nods, like she's turning over the words.

She's not comfortable now. I can tell that by how quickly she's breathing and how she grips the hem of her coat so tight her knuckles have gone very pale.

I want to reach out and tell her it's okay to come out to me.

But she doesn't know I know. She doesn't know I'm who she's been speaking to on the helpline. And this is where I should say it—where I should confess. I know that.

But I can't. Something just stops me.

"In any case," I say, at last. "Aceness is...it varies. From person to person, but also sometimes within the same person. Sometimes I feel more demi—it's all a spectrum anyway."

Sophie nods and stirs the spoon in her mug. The milky coffee swirls round and round.

I search for a new topic of conversation—her ex is definitely off limits, and something tells me not to ask her about work. Not with the whole book fiasco. Instead, I blurt out about my washing machine—about how it's broken but I've ordered new parts for it.

"Okay," she says, looking a bit lost.

"I mean, it's really inconvenient. I've got laundry piled up in my room, all just waiting to get washed, and I can't even do it yet."

Why the hell am I rambling about my washing machine and dirty laundry? I breathe deeply, trying to think fast. I need a better topic of conversation that this.

I ask her which bands she likes, and soon we're talking and laughing.

Surprisingly, she likes the same ones as me—and this is weird, talking and even laughing with her as she tells me how she and two friends from uni went to see one of the bands and how she'd fallen in some mud on the way there and had had to go there, looking worst for wear.

"I'd just had my hair done too, like half an hour before, as Maisie'd just qualified as a hairdresser. So, she'd done my hair, and Kate's too. And I literally got mud all down this side of my face, all my hair ruined. And it got in my bra too, because I was wearing this really low-cut top. It was so embarrassing."

"Embarrassing—well, I've got a story there," I say, and I tell her about taking my wet laundry on the bus and how the woman thought I'd had an accident.

"No way." Sophie gasps, her eyes wide. "Seriously? She actually said that?"

"Uh-huh." I nod.

We both descend into giggles, and when the waiter asks if we want another coffee and hot chocolate, we agree. And this—this *is* fun. It really is. It reminds me of the early days at St. Bridget's—how we'd compete against each other, but still be smiling.

I've never told anyone this, but in Year Seven, I was convinced that Sophie and I would become good friends. I'd never have anticipated what she and her friends would do in Year Eleven. And just thinking about that now dampens my mood a little.

Still, it was Janey, right? Not Sophie.

"Well, this was fun," Sophie says, when at last we decide we'd better get back to my apartment.

I need to do some work, and Mrs. Dalton should be up by now. Sophie says they need to go to the police station together.

"We should do this again sometime," Sophie says. "It's nice to have a friend."

A friend. She thinks of me as a friend. And I don't know why that makes me feel so warm inside. But also so guilty. Because friends don't keep secrets. Friends don't deceive. And that's exactly what I'm doing.

TWENTY-FIVE

Sophie

THREE DAYS LATER, Victoria, Martin, and I are allowed to move back in. The police have taken countless statements from all of us, and I've given them all the info about Adam that I can think of—even if the most important thing, his current address, is something I don't know.

Back in Victoria's spare room, I rearrange my belongings. The police didn't clear everything up like I expected they would, and I've spent the last two hours straightening things out. Still got no laptop though.

I send a quick text to Courtney, asking her if the prank contest is still going ahead. When Zara heard of the break-in she'd put a pause on the game while we all got sorted. I was surprised at that, because I would've thought that Courtney and I living in the same house made for the perfect opportunity for us to prank each other.

But I was also relieved. I can't deny that. Knowing that I could relax at Courtney's was huge. And really, she was pretty nice, all things considered. She said she doesn't normally eat eggs, but she went out and bought half a dozen so I could stick to my meal plan. I wouldn't have expected her to be so considerate, all things considered.

But she was.

She is.

We'd made the coffee at the café a regular thing during my stay with her—except we did it in the late afternoon, after Courtney had finished work—and I really hope we're doing it today too, as I've actually found I look forward to it. Not just because the coffee at that café is amazing, but also because I've found I like talking to Courtney. She's interesting. And her face is so expressive. It sounds weird even focusing on it, and I don't know how I didn't realize before, but when she talks about something she's really passionate about, she gets animated. Her eyes are wide and her whole countenance and expressions just add this extra level.

My phone buzzes. *The prank war is back on*, Courtney says.

I smile and reply. *How's work going?*

Time seems to slow down as I wait for her reply. A minute passes. Then two, three, four. Ten, fifteen, twenty. And the whole time I'm just staring at my phone, waiting.

"Get a grip," I mutter, because this isn't like me. Even when I was best friends with Janey, Rebecca, and Stacey, I never wasted time waiting for them to reply to my texts. Well, they all replied instantly really, but I'm sure I wouldn't have reacted like this. So sure of it. So why am I now?

I decide to busy myself with reading, only I can't concentrate on the book, because I keep checking my phone. And this is ridiculous. This is—

My phone pings.

I snatch it to me in an instant, clicking onto Courtney's message.

Good, thanks. Bit boring. Just contacting surveyors today and negotiating fees.

I type back: *Wow, that does sound boring. Want to get a coffee later?*

The three dots show that she's typing, and I wait with baited breath.

Sorry, I've got something on later, and at the weekend, but I can do Monday evening.

I tell her that would be great, and I send a cute meme as an extra reply, but I can't help but be curious about what she's doing tonight and at the weekend. Monday seems like ages away.

"I think it would be helpful," Tabitha says, "if you talked to someone close to you about it all. You've said you feel like you're keeping a secret, and it's this secrecy about your sexuality that could be contributing toward these feelings of shame that you describe—feelings that were planted by your ex."

I nod and breathe deeply. Tabitha's on speaker phone, and the apartment's empty. I picture Victoria coming home and me telling her. I do need to tell someone that I think I'm ace, someone who I actually know in person, and I think Tabitha's right that doing so will help me feel less ashamed of it.

"But I literally can't think of anyone who I could tell," I say. "I'm not ready to tell my step-mum yet. I'm worried about her reaction, and I don't want the first person I tell to have a bad reaction."

"That's perfectly understandable," Tabitha says. "So, what about friends? Other family members?"

"I guess there are a few friends from uni," I say. "I do talk to them every now and again. Mainly online. I mean, I could tell them. But it's just… I don't know. I'm still trying to figure it out myself."

"Then wait until you've sorted it out in your head a bit more," she advises. "You'll know when the time is right."

"Will I?"

"You will."

I smile and we end the call. I feel better after talking to her, that's for sure.

Half an hour later, my phone buzzes with a text, and next to my ear, it nearly makes me jump. A text—from Adam?

I swallow hard and feel a bit nauseous. Is this where he confirms that he did arrange the break-in?

But it's not him. It's Courtney.

She's only sent a meme this time. It makes me smile though and I send another back. And thus starts a conversation between the two of us, consisting entirely of memes and GIFs, and I can't stop smiling.

TWENTY-SIX

Courtney

NORMALLY, I LOOK forward to the weekend, but this one is just chaotic. I do the essential food shopping, chase Sergeant Ginger Paws out of my apartment twice, and meet my mother for lunch on the Saturday, where she tells me about the politics of her latest book club. I refrain from telling her any more about Sophie—or how we're meeting up Monday evening. That feels like a secret I want to keep close to my heart, something just for me that makes me smile.

On Sunday morning, I set aside several hours to catch up on some of the work I got behind on before, after the break-in on the Dalton's place, and by that afternoon, I've caught up nicely. I also receive an email from John asking if I can work on Monday and swap around my day off.

No problem, I email him back.

Both the weekend evenings, I also work at the center. On Sunday evening, Peter calls in sick, and it would be the one night when we're suddenly really busy. A surprising number really. Most of them are decent though, not too many acephobic 'worried' parents on the line. Only one woman who wonders if her son needs to see a doctor.

"It's just not normal for a man not to be interested in sex!" she wails, and she's got one of those screeching, high-pitched voices. "There must be something wrong with him. Some illness or something."

"There's nothing wrong with experiencing no sexual attraction," I say. "Asexuality isn't something pathological, or something that needs fixing."

Really, we probably get these calls the most, and each time, it's so draining—because these people who think that asexuality needs to be cured are just relentless. They seemingly have a never-ending supply of energy to fuel into their beliefs, and on more than one occasion, I've been read a pretty well-written—albeit ill-informed—article that they've written especially for this call, as they try and persuade me that actually there *is* something wrong with all ace people and that we need to be cured. Half the time, I just want to scream down the phone, "We don't need to be cured! We are not broken!" But I've got to be professional and all that.

By the time my shift is over, I'm exhausted.

Dylan phones when I'm on the bus, and he asks me if I want to go around for pizza tomorrow evening.

"Sorry." I wince. "I can't. I said I'd meet Sophie for a coffee then. We're trying that new place. You know the one that's open in the evening and does nights? Really expensive, on the main street."

"Wait." He's frowning, I can tell. "Wait, you're going on a date with Sophie?"

"It's not a date," I say. "It's friends. That's all."

"Nah," he says. "That place is notorious for couples. The clue is in the name. *Coffee Couple*. Courtney, you—who judged what I was reading because it's a bully romance—are now dating your bully."

"No, it's not a date," I say firmly. "We're just friends."

He snorts. "Well, at least Zara's going to be there, filming, right? I take it you've contacted *Coffee Couple* about that to check it's okay?"

"Uh, no," I say. "Zara's not going to be there. No filming."

Dylan inhales sharply. "Zara's going to be gutted to miss out on drama."

"This isn't drama."

"Well, anyway, Court, you can't go out with Sophie. Not on a date. You can't actually be living a bully romance here."

"Exactly, and I'm not. It's unhealthy. Precisely what I was saying about your book."

"Look those books are just fun. Escapism. No real-life consequences for the readers. But what you're doing isn't like that. It's real. And you can't get together with Sophie. You should just stick to the prank stuff and nothing more."

But even thinking about that, I'm not sure I can now. Just seeing how upset Sophie was after the break in, and how she confided in me that she feels violated since it, I feel like I can hardly resume the game. Maybe we can get Zara to put a permanent stop to it.

And well, I don't think I want to scare Sophie now. I mean, I don't want her to move away. I mean, sure, if she was still the girl she'd been at school, then I'd have no problems, but she seems so different now. She's grown up.

Sophie is different. That much is clear. She's not the same person she once was. At school, she was a nightmare, always having to prove she was better than everyone else. She was sharp-tongued and mean, and she and her friends went out of the way to make certain individuals' lives hell.

But now she's calmer. I've heard so many people say that the wild ones calm down after school, that people mature. And I'd assumed 'wild ones' only covered those who were just disruptive at school. Not the bullies.

But Sophie is different. She's nicer. And I like her.

TWENTY-SEVEN

Courtney

THE NEXT MORNING, an hour before I'm due to leave for the office, the new parts I ordered for my washing machine arrive by courier—about time! And this is perfect! I can get to work, have time when I get back to sort out the machine, and then get out to *Coffee Couple* to meet Sophie.

Quickly, I unpack the box and I rub my hands together as I stare at the different components—then realize the gleeful motion probably makes me look like a cartoon. I mean, I have a bit of a complex about that ever since Ray from work—he's one of the senior designers—said I look and act like a cartoon. Always lively. He meant it kindly, but it does make me wonder if sometimes I'm not taken seriously.

I head out to work and arrive at the same time as Sally.

"Didn't know you were in today?" she says.

I nod. "Last-minute change really. Are you okay?"

She looks exhausted, huge bags under her eyes. "The library project is just a nightmare," she says. "You're lucky the boss didn't put you on it too. Ended up taking work home with me last night, and you know how much I hate that. And taking up the whole weekend too!"

"Well, it'll be over soon, right?"

"Not soon enough."

I give her my most sympathetic smile before I head to the back room to grab my hardhat and high-vis jacket. Paul and I are visiting the construction site today for the new leisure center to make some final tweaks to the plans given to us by the clients. Apparently, they contacted the boss on Saturday morning and said they wanted some big changes done to the plans already made. There's not really a lot of time for flexibility now, not at this stage, so I guess that's why my day off has been changed.

After the visit, I'm back in the office, working on sketches and visual reference guides for my two other projects—a woman who's remodeling her bungalow to make it more wheelchair accessible, and a private school that wants to redesign the interior of a proposed building. The latter one is a client that was originally allocated to Paul, but apparently his designs were never approved. He'd wished me luck with this one—and warned me that the private school's management has a habit of being awkward. Oh, and I need to collect the new fabric samples too. A new range came out last week, and I may as well get those in today rather than tomorrow.

All in all, it's a busy day, and by the time I'm finished, I'm nearly half asleep on the bus back home. Still, fitting the new parts for the washing machine will wake me up—and if that doesn't, my nervousness over meeting Sophie later will. And I don't even know why I'm nervous—I haven't been nervous any of the other days we've done this.

Only we haven't done *this*—it's always just been coffee in the mornings before. But this, well, this is dinnertime, so presumably we're going to be eating too. And I think of what Dylan said—how it's a date.

I scrunch my face up. I mean, it isn't—is it?

In my kitchen, I focus on the washing machine challenge, use it as a distraction from the way I definitely have butterflies in my tummy.

Pulling the seal and various spring devices out of the old machine is easy. Fitting the new one is not, no matter how many YouTube videos I watch.

"Oh my god," I huff, an hour later. "My hands literally aren't strong enough for this."

I call Dylan, and he arrives half an hour later, Jack in toe, with a big, fancy toolbox.

"Where's Kayla?" I ask.

"My mum's got her," Dylan says. "And I thought you had that date tonight?" He raises his eyebrows.

"It's not a date."

Dylan snorts. He looks at Jack. "Well, we better try and fix this thing. Wouldn't want you to be late, Court."

After a long, long time, and lots of swearing, Dylan and Jack get the seal in place.

"Now to try it," I say, and the sense of accomplishment has me beaming, even if the men did the hard work. "See, this is so much better than buying a new one. Saved money and we've had this cool catch-up."

Neither Dylan nor Jack look convinced.

I plug the machine back in and set a rinse cycle, with the machine empty. Water dribbles down the inside of the door. I frown. The stream is weak, barely a trickle. It's practically not there at all.

"Think you need more water than that to wash the clothes," Dylan says.

"It'll do it in a minute," I say, drumming my fingers against my thighs, praying that more water will appear. "Just wait."

And as if on cue, the machine suddenly gushes with water. It sprays into the drum, filling it rapidly and—

Water sloshes out the bottom, leaking from under the machine.

"Holy sheep," I mutter. Frustration pours into me.

Jack jolts back. "Must be the outer drum in it. Must have a hole."

"Should've just got a new one," Dylan says. "Like I said from the start."

By the time I get to *Coffee Couple*, I'm late—more outrageously late than fashionably late—and I'm soaked. I changed out of my work clothes hastily before leaving—they were splattered with soapy water anyway—and tried to wrangle a brush through my hair a little, only for it to get stuck. Properly stuck. I'd had to plead and beg with the brush to get it to part company with my hair.

Sophie's at a table by the window, and she waves at me as I arrive. And—

Oh my God. It's romantic. Candlelight—freaking actual candles on the table. And flowers. A gentle melody fills the air, and I look around at the other customers. All of them are obviously couples. A man in his sixties holds hands with a woman who looks slightly younger than him, their arms stretched across the table to one another. Another couple sits near Sophie, staring into each other's eyes.

My throat tightens.

"Sorry I'm late," I mumble, and I'm surprised I even manage to get the words out, given all my brain screams is *Is this a date?*

"No worries," Sophie says.

A waiter comes over and asks what we'd like to drink. "We now have the early Valentine's promotion running," he says. "Which is a half-price bottle of any of our wines."

Seems early for a Valentine's promotion. It's only the 26th January. But, well, I suppose this place is romantic. I look at Sophie, feeling my face redden—because she does look pretty.

"Great, we'll have that," Sophie says, and the waiter says he'll be back shortly to take our order and hurries away.

"This is, uh, formal," I say.

Sophie grins as she leans back. "I had no idea it was like this inside—honestly, they're going to think we're a couple or something." She laughs.

I laugh, then I wonder if my laugh sounds natural. Is it too loud? Too high-pitched? Does it sound forced? I stop laughing.

"Whoa, this menu is…" Sophie frowns, looking at her menu. "I assumed it would just be coffee…but I'm guessing you haven't eaten? Do you want to get dinner?"

Dinner? Dinner with Sophie? I look at my menu. "Uh, sure." My eyes glaze over. "I have no idea what any of this is."

"Maybe that first one is potato?" she suggests.

I look around for the waiter. "I think I need a translator for this."

When the waiter returns, if he's bemused by our lack of understanding of the menu, he doesn't show it. He calmly explains it all, but then I'm not even sure what it is that I end up ordering.

"So, how've you been?" I ask Sophie once the waiter's left, because it's too quiet and I need conversation—and if I don't get her to lead it, I'm going to end up talking about my washing machine again.

She smiles. "Well, okay." She pulls on her hair. As usual, it looks perfect. She glances around behind her, then at me.

"What is it?" I ask.

"The thing is," Sophie says. "There's something I've been wanting to talk to you about for a while. And I keep thinking now would be the perfect time."

"Okay?" I frown.

"You... I don't even know how to say it. I've only come out to one person before, and…and it was easy with her because she didn't know me. But you do know me—and all what happened between us before... God, you've no idea how bad I feel about that now. Like maybe I made your life hell because I knew I was like you."

"You're...ace too?" I manage to keep my voice neutral, and I pray I'm not going to suddenly say too much and let her know that I already knew.

Slowly, Sophie nods. "I still feel really... I don't know. Embarrassed?"

"It's nothing to be embarrassed by," I say.

"Yeah, that's what Tabitha says. She's this person who works on a helpline. Places for Aces. It's a charity."

I nod, feeling heat flush my face. Now is the time to do it, to come clean. But still something stops me. "I think I've heard of them. The charity."

"They're so great," Sophie says. "And Tabitha's suggested that I come out to a close friend or someone."

"So, that's me?" I raise my eyebrows.

Sophie nods. "I hope you don't mind. I just couldn't think of anyone else. And of course you get it."

I breathe out a long breath. So that's what this meal was about. It's not a date. She's not interested in me romantically. She just wanted to follow Tabitha's advice.

"Thanks," Sophie says. "It just feels easier, friendlier, you know?"

"Yeah," I say, and I pretend that my heart isn't aching as we talk—just as friends.

TWENTY-EIGHT

Sophie

VICTORIA'S STILL UP when I get back to the apartment, and I join her on the sofa.

"Nice evening?" she asks.

"Yeah," I say. "We went to *Coffee Couple*."

"*We?*" She raises her eyebrows.

"Me and Courtney."

"I'm so glad you two are getting on well now," she says. "It's important to have friends."

Huh. Don't I know it?

Victoria's curled up on the sofa, but she shifts over a little bit, giving me more room. I smile, and I wonder if now's the time. Should I tell her about me being ace?

I mean, it's just the two of us—though it often is. Martin comes and goes pretty much as he pleases. But now feels like a good time—and I feel confident, having just talked through my feelings and my identity with Courtney.

I take a deep breath. "Can I tell you something?"

Victoria tilts her head toward me and reaches for my hand. "Of course. What is it?"

My heart's pounding, and it suddenly feels so hot in here. "There's just... There's something I want to tell you. Something personal. About me."

She gives me an encouraging smile, but I can see she's wary too.

I swallow hard, my heart now apparently pounding in my throat. It makes me feel nauseous.

"You're like the only parent I've got now," I say, "and I... I've been doing a lot of thinking the last few weeks because I think I'm...asexual."

Just saying the word out loud to her is a massive relief. As cliché as it sounds, it really does feel like a weight being lifted from my shoulders.

Victoria's eyes widen. "Asexual?" She repeats my word as if it's something completely foreign and she's not sure she's pronouncing it correctly. "You want to be celibate?"

"It's different," I say. "Celibacy is a choice. This is...more who I am?"

And I'm looking at her, waiting for her to say something— but she doesn't. She just frowns and stares at me. So, I speak.

"I... I don't experience sexual attraction. And being asexual is... There are a lot of people who are ace. That's the term for those who are asexual. It's a spectrum, and I've talked to a couple people about it."

"People?" Victoria's frown gets deeper.

"Courtney," I say. "And I called this helpline."

"Oh, baby." She pats my hand. "You should've just told me, and I could've booked you a doctor's appointment."

"What?" I stare at her.

"Well, to discuss this—it must be linked to something, and these people that run these helplines, you never know who they are. You need to make sure they're credible, if you're going to be paying them."

"Paying them?"

"To fix it," she says. "Really, Fifi, you should've just told me, and we could've spoken to a doctor for free. Or if the NHS can't help with that, we could've found a respectable private doctor. Not some voice on the end of a telephone."

I feel like I've been punched. "Fix it?" I whisper. My stomach churns, and suddenly I feel sick. I wish I hadn't eaten so much at the meal with Courtney. I was careful—only ordering salad, but it came out drenched in dressing, and just the sight of it made me uneasy. "There's nothing to fix—I'm not broken."

"Fifi." She squeezes my hand tighter, and I want more than anything to pull it away, but I don't. I just stare at her. "Don't worry," she says. "I'll get you a doctor's appointment first thing in the morning. I'll go with you. It's probably something hormonal, or to do with stress. We'll sort this out—I mean, to not be interested in sex, after a break-up like you've had is normal. None of this means you're…asexual."

"No, you don't understand. I've always felt like this."

"It just means Adam was never right for you or your hormones are out of whack," she says. "But you'll meet someone who is, and you'll get over this…blip."

She thinks it's a blip. She thinks my sexuality is a blip. A problem. Something that needs to be fixed. I gulp and gulp as I retreat to the spare room in the evening and call Places for Aces.

The line rings, but when it's answered it's a male voice.

"Uh, is Tabitha there?" I ask, and I'm struggling to keep it together.

"Sorry, Tabitha doesn't work this evening," the man says. "But can I help?"

He tells me his name, but I'm not listening or concentrating. I can't just talk to a stranger about this. I can't!

"When's Tabitha working again?" I ask. My voice cracks. "I've had several conversations with her already. I'd prefer to stick with her."

"Let me just check the rota, dear," he says. There's a long pause. "Ah, yes. She's in tomorrow. Starts at six o'clock."

"Thank you," I whisper. "Can you tell her to expect me to call? My name's Sophie. She'll know who I am."

He says he will, and I end the call and dissolve into tears.

How can this have all gone so wrong? How can—

There's a knock on my door, and I jump.

"Fifi?"

I sniff loudly. "I'm going to bed," I call back, my voice thick. The words are partially obscured by my tears.

"Oh, Fifi, don't cry," Victoria says, pushing open my door. "We'll get you sorted, I promise."

Get me sorted? There's nothing to sort. I gulp, and I want to scream those words. But I don't. I'm quiet. Just sitting here.

"I think you should come back into the living room with me," Victoria says. "We can watch a film. Take your mind off things."

Yeah, take my mind off how I'm broken. Because what if she is right? My mind spins. What if I'm just scarred by what Adam did, how he treated me all the time, and just think that

I'm ace because of that? What if I'm clutching at straws, trying to find somewhere I belong? Because that's all I really want: somewhere to belong.

TWENTY-NINE

Sophie

I SIT DOWN by my mother's grave. The grass is a little long, and it tickles my bare legs. I've come straight from school, didn't tell anyone I was coming here because I didn't really know that I was.

Not until I got here.

I reach out and trace the letters on the gravestone. GEORGINA SWAY.

"Sway," I say. My last name used to annoy me—I used to hate it. It sounded like a joke name or something. But, now, it's my connection to my mother. She and I have the same name. She and Dad weren't married when I was born, and everyone apparently questioned why I wasn't Sophie Dalton.

I breathe deeply. People say you should feel close to the deceased loved one when at their grave. But I don't—or maybe I do, when I keep gravitating here—but it's not like how I thought it would be.

The first time I visited, I half expected to hear her voice, smell her perfume, maybe even see her. Like an apparition or something. But none of those things happened. It was just me sitting here, staring at the gravestone. I laid one single white rose across the grass in front of it—a rose I'd plucked from St. Bridget's gardens earlier that day.

I've brought a rose today too—also from the school gardens. No one saw me take it, and my mother loved those roses. On the days when she visited—before the visit that killed her—she always remarked on the roses.

I clutched that rose tightly to me on the train here today. The ticket inspector gave me a funny look, but he didn't say anything about it. Maybe he thought some boy had given it to me, that I was a lovesick teen.

I always wonder if I should talk to Mum when I'm here. Because that's what people do on TV and in films. In books, too. They talk and update the person on the things that are happening—but I can't bring myself to do it. I never can. I'd feel too self-conscious, just talking out loud, to myself.

So I just sit here. Sit in the grass, staring at the rose and the gravestone.

I sit here—alone.

Every time I come here, my father's never here. I don't think he's even visited this church again, not since the funeral. But he likes to pretend she's still alive. Coming here would ruin that illusion.

For a long time, I've wondered if maybe my mother's parents—my grandparents—will show up. If this will be how I meet them. The other Sways—people I've never met.

But they never turn up.

Dad told me they'd disowned my mother when she'd started her relationship with him.

I don't know why.

I don't know anything about them.

The sun begins to come out, warms my skin, and I breathe deeply. I think about what my mother might say if she was sitting here with me. She'd be chattering away about the latest book she was reading and how she was still determined to finish the one she'd started writing.

And then she'd tell me that I should follow my dreams and not leave it so late, like she did.

"You're a creator too," she told me once. "A writer, an actress—you could do both. You've got the heart for it, and you have to follow your heart."

I breathe deeply and smile a little. Then I look at the time. I have to go, have to get the train back to St. Bridget's.

I stand up. My legs ache, like they don't want me to go.

"Bye, Mum," I whisper.

THIRTY

Courtney

I BARELY MAKE it in time from work to the center. The office was hectic today—our books are already pretty much full, and yet the boss has taken on three more 'small' projects. Told us to fit them in somehow.

I've been in meetings with planners and surveyors all day, given the building I've been allocated is a grade two listed property and the client wants the inside completely remodeled. So, my head's spinning by the time I'm sitting in the chair with my headset on.

And it's busy tonight. There are three of us manning the phones, and usually when this happens we get some time where we can just chat. I like Tammy and Kendra, and we always have a little catch-up—only tonight, the phones ring nonstop.

"Hello, this is Places for Aces. My name is Tabitha. How can I help you?"

The sound of quick breathing fills the line. "I... This is a bit…personal. But you can talk about, uh, being ace, right?"

"Uh, yes," I say. "Do you have any questions."

"Well. Yeah. I'm just. I'm worried. My name's Blake, and I'm still transitioning—to male."

"To clarify, you mean you are medically transitioning? As you've always been male."

"Yeah," he says. "Medically transitioning. And I identify as asexual at the moment, and being ace is a huge part of my identity. Like I'm in this Facebook group for aces, and it's so, so important to me, this whole community. But I'm also friends with a couple guys who've transitioned recently and they've told me as soon as they started their masculinizing hormone therapy—you know, T, uh, testosterone—their sex drive increased massively. They're not ace, though, but I don't know, I'm just worried. Like what if when I start it, it means I'm not ace anymore? I've done so much advocating work for the ace spectrum and I've actually been so worried I'm barely sleeping. Because what if people then say that I'm not ace once I'm on T, and then they say I was lying about being ace all along, just to get attention? Because like, the work I've done has got me several interviews and I have a business around creating ace-meme t-shirts. And I'm just worried I'm going to feel like a massive fraud."

"Hey, it's okay, Blake," I say, and as I speak, I navigate to a folder on the computer. Mrs. Mitchell put together a list of resources, and we've got several on HRT. "Having testosterone may increase your sex drive—it affects everyone differently—but even if it does, it doesn't necessarily mean you won't be ace. There are plenty of asexual individuals with high libidos and sex-drives—and they're still ace. Having a high sex drive doesn't mean that you can't be ace, if the way that you experience sexual attraction doesn't change."

"I just… I'm worried," he says. "I just, I don't want to lose part of my identity, just when this whole process is helping me live like who I actually am."

"I understand that," I say. *There*. I find the article by Calvin Kasulke that I'm looking for and scan it quickly. I've read every article, study, and blog post in Mrs. Mitchell's database, and I often have the relevant ones open when on a call. "So, there is the possibility that things *could* change." Kasulke's article references how, in a study, 40% of trans men and 49% of transmascs experienced a change in their sexuality. "I feel it's important to note that, Blake, because you're right, in that it can happen. And if it does, that's okay—many people experience changes in their sexuality. It's normal, and I don't want you to be worrying about it. And, remember, asexuality *is* a spectrum. It includes gray-ace, fray, and demi, along with others—so even if your sexuality does change, you could still be part of the ace spectrum. The term 'asexual' will still be yours to claim if you want it, even if HRT does increase your sex drive or the way you experience sexual attraction. No one can tell you that you aren't ace, just because you'll be having this hormone therapy, if that's how you still identify."

I do my best to reassure him and suggest that perhaps phoning us regularly as he's undergoing the HRT would be helpful, once he knows how the T is—or isn't—affecting things. As we end the call, I think I've helped. Or at least, I hope I have. Sometimes, being part of this helpline feels like a huge responsibility, and many a time I've worried for hours after a call. What if I said slightly the wrong thing?

The phone rings again, and I answer it.

"Hello? Tabitha?" It's Sophie's voice—but she sounds strange. Her voice is thick and—

She's been crying.

I freeze. "What's wrong?"

She sniffs and gulps. It sounds like she's still crying now. The messy kind of crying. "I told my step-mum about being ace, and… She's making me see a doctor," she says. "Tomorrow. It was supposed to be today, but they had no slots left today. So, I've got one for tomorrow. And I can't get out of the appointment. It's a private one she's booked, as an emergency, and she thinks this is something that can be fixed. And now I'm all just, like, wondering if she's right. What if I am broken?"

"Oh, Sophie," I say. "Take a deep breath. Okay? Yeah, and another deep breath." I lean forward in my seat. "You're not broken, okay? I promise you're not broken."

"But she thinks I am."

"And some people do think this," I say—but I'd never have imagined that Mrs. Dalton was one of them. "And that's why we need to educate them."

"I can't get out of going to this appointment tomorrow," I say. "I asked her to cancel it, and she said I was being ungrateful. I've got no choice."

"You've always got a choice. You're an adult."

She sniffs louder, and my ear's filled with the sound.

"Is there anyone who could go with you to the appointment tomorrow, other than your step-mother?" I ask. "Someone to fight your corner, kind of thing? Moral support can be very reassuring."

"I don't know," she says.

"No friends?" I prompt, because I'd go with her—I'd go with her in a heartbeat. But she doesn't know it's me she's speaking to, and I need her to address me about it directly.

"Well, there is someone," she says. "A friend. I could ask her, but I don't know… I keep telling myself that maybe the doctor will agree that asexuality is a thing, that it doesn't need to be fixed anyway."

I nod. "Yes, that would of course be the desired outcome."

"Thank you, uh, I've got to go now," she says suddenly. "But, Tabitha, I'm so glad I've got you. You've no idea how much you've helped me. Especially at the beginning of all this—it felt like you were the only person in the world who understands."

"I'm glad I've been able to help," I say.

Tell her! The voice in my head screams.

But then she hangs up, and it's too late.

I wait and wait for Sophie to contact me—to contact me as Courtney, not Tabitha—and tell me what's going on. I wait for my phone to ring, for her to ask me to go to the appointment with her. And I'll drop everything. I've already told John I'll take Friday as my day off this week, but I could change it around. Make it tomorrow, Wednesday, instead.

All I know is that I have to be there for her. I have to. I've just got this fierce feeling in my heart that I need to do all I can here—and give Mrs. Dalton a piece of mind. Because she can't say things like that, and especially not to Sophie. The teenage Sophie could've handled it, maybe, but today's Sophie is more sensitive, more unsure. And I need to protect her.

But my phone doesn't ring. It doesn't ring all evening, or during the night, and the next morning I watch the minutes on the clock tick by. It's nearly time for me to leave for work, and I contemplate marching upstairs and getting Sophie to invite me along. Only I can't do that without raising suspicion about how I know.

Sighing, I grab my bag and keys. Guess it looks like I am going into work.

———

At work, I check my phone religiously—so much so that Sally questions me about it.

"I'm just worried about a friend," I say.

"That Sophie woman?" she asks, raising her eyebrows.

"What? No. How did you know?" Flustered, I spin in my chair so I'm facing her desk.

"Because you mention her all the time, and now you're obviously anxious about something. Come on, spill."

But I can't—I can't do that, not without outing Sophie to Sally. The two may not have spoken since that awkward meal, but I know how it feels to be outed, and I'm not going to do that to Sophie. It's wrong, and she's going through enough as it is.

At lunch time, my phone rings, and I snatch it to my ear in an instance. "Hello?"

"Courtney." It's Zara's voice, and I feel myself deflate. "Just checking in because you've not sent me any pranks," she says. "I mean neither's Sophie—so it's not a problem as such, and I've just been editing all the footage. I think I've got enough for the earlier rounds, because we can doctor it and just do some more interviews with you—that could be done later today, if you're free? No? Oh, well tomorrow then? The evening? I'll see if Sophie is free then, too. And I also want to do the final round prep too, when I've got you both. If we can get something that tops all the others, that would be great."

"Great," I echo her, but there's no enthusiasm in my voice.

"Court, what's wrong?"

"Nothing. I'm just at work and it's busy. I've got to go."

I feel bad lying, but I do need to keep my phone free in case Sophie calls. I bite my lip as I stare at my phone once again. It's almost one o'clock now. Is she having the appointment right now? Or already had it? Or have it looming ahead?

I can barely concentrate on my work I'm so nervous. There's a good chance she's had that appointment now, and the thought of her going through something like that alone, where she's being taken to a doctor in order to be 'cured' of her sexuality, just makes me so angry.

I decide to take a break at two o'clock and call her—I mean, I'm her friend. Friends check in anyway, don't they?

I scroll to her contact and—

My phone buzzes. Her name fills the screen. She's calling me.

Sophie Sway is calling me.

THIRTY-ONE

Sophie

"PLEASE, COURTNEY," I whisper. "Please, can you come and get me? Things have gone wrong with Victoria and…" I pause because my voice is crackling, and I can't be speaking too loudly.

I take a deep breath and look around the toilet stall. It's small, and shutting myself in here, instead of sitting in the waiting room with Victoria was all I could think of to do. But I've already been in here for a while, and she's going to come looking for me.

"Where are you?" Courtney asks.

I give her the name of the clinic and tell her to hurry. I know Courtney in Exeter, but my appointment is in ten minutes. And realistically, I know that she's not going to get here before then—that's if she can just walk out of her job right this second. What if her boss stops her?

Back out in the waiting room, Victoria makes a joke about me doing a runner. There are lines around her eyes—tension. She hasn't slept well the last two nights. Neither have I.

"And have we got a Sophie Sway?" A bright-eyed nurse pokes her head out of the door opposite, beaming away.

"Yes, that's us," Victoria says. "Well, that's my step-daughter. Not literally both of us." She laughs her forced, uncomfortable laugh.

"The doctor's ready for you now," the nurse says.

My legs feel too soft, insubstantial, as I make my way to the doctor's office. My heart's pounding and sweat drips down my back. Victoria's right behind me.

"Are you okay with your step-mother being here?" the doctor asks me. She's an elegant looking woman, but she has a kind face.

I glance back at Victoria.

"I think it's best if I am present in this appointment," Victoria says.

"Sophie?" the doctor prompts, raising her eyebrows.

I nod.

The door shuts. The seat I sit in is too soft. I'm sinking too much.

"And how can I help?" the doctor asks. Her name badge says she's called Dr. James.

Victoria does the talking, explaining my 'big secret' to the doctor, talking about asexuality as if it's something shameful. My head spins the whole time, and tears keep filling my eyes and overflowing.

Dr. James listens and nods, makes thinking noises. "It's probably just a hormonal issue," she says. "But it's also normal to be a bit depressed after a relationship ends. Many people don't feel sexually attracted to other people straight away. This just sounds like it's a bit of a difficult time for you."

A difficult time? I'm not depressed over the breakup with Adam. I'm relieved. Even if I am scared about his threats—

but those are empty, right? He didn't break into our apartment, because he would've done some sort of follow-up on that by now, right? He would've made sure to let me know it was him. But he hasn't... So, it was just a coincidence. A random robbery.

And I'm not depressed! I think of Courtney and how happy I've been the last few days with her. At the coffee shops, at that meal.

"It may be very helpful to speak to a therapist or counsellor about this," Dr. James says. "It could very well be down to a lack of self-confidence and self-esteem."

I look up at her. "You don't believe asexuality exists?"

"I believe there are people who use that term to describe how they're feeling—such as how you're feeling now—but it's a dangerous term."

"A dangerous term?"

"It implies it's okay to feel that way," Dr. James says.

"But it *is* okay!" I exclaim. I blink. This can't be happening. She can't actually be saying that.

Dr. James shakes her head. "In my experience, people claim to be asexual if they're actually attracted to the same sex but they feel ashamed about it. Or they claim to be asexual if they're scared of physical intimacy. It becomes a defense mechanism."

"No, it's *real*." I grit my teeth. "There's loads of stuff online about it."

"You shouldn't believe everything you read online," Dr. James says. "Now, I'll arrange some blood tests for you to check your sex hormones. The nurse can take your blood right after this appointment. We have a phlebotomy room just down the corridor. I think it's also worth me referring you to a counsellor to tackle these issues of self-esteem."

I don't say anything. Victoria mumbles a thank-you.

"Don't worry, Sophie." Dr. James smiles as we stand to leave. "We'll get you fixed."

I'm not broken.

But I don't say the words. I don't say anything as I walk out of the room, out of the whole building, without getting the blood drawn, ignoring Victoria's shouts.

THIRTY-TWO

Courtney

"SHE DID WHAT?" I stare at Sophie, my heart pounding.

We're sitting on a bench in the park, and Sophie keeps wiping her eyes as she tells me what the doctor said.

"Seriously?" I shake my head. "She can't get away with this. I'm going to write to her."

"Write to her?" Sophie blinks.

I nod. "She needs educating—she can't say that stuff. Hell, I've a good mind to go around there now." I breathe deeply, but I can feel my nostrils flaring in a way that always makes me feel unattractive.

"I'm just glad you're here," Sophie says—and she reaches out and takes my hand in hers.

Electricity runs through me, and I stare at our joined hands between us on the bench.

She squeezes my fingers. "Thank you."

"I'm just sorry I didn't get there in time," I say, and I could kick myself for not being there. Hell, I knew this appointment was happening. I should've made sure I could get there quickly.

Only I didn't know where or when it was until Sophie phoned. Realistically, I couldn't have done anything more unless I'd confessed to her that I am Tabitha.

"I'm dreading going home," Sophie says.

"Then stay at mine," I say. It's simple. Sophie needs to be with people who respect her—not who take her to the doctors like that. "I mean, I haven't got a working washing machine yet—you wouldn't believe the fiasco with that—but there's a launderette down the road and also I've been doing some of mine at…at work." Just in time, I remember not to mention the charity center.

Sophie's eyes light up. "I could?"

"Yeah, of course."

She makes a considering sound, then nods. "I can sleep on the sofa this time though."

"It's fine," I say, and I can feel the change in me. How it feels like my soul is going to burst. Because this is Sophie— and I want her to be at my house. I want to be around her as much as possible.

I jolt.

This isn't right. I can't be developing feelings, to this extent, for Sophie. She made my teen years hell.

This isn't some bully romance story. And I hate those anyway. What person in their right mind would fall in love with a person who made them so miserable? It's such a cliché, and those films and books where it happens just send the wrong message. It's not healthy for someone to be in love with their bully.

Wait. *Love*? Who said anything about love?

And she wasn't the bully—that was Janey.

And Sophie's different now. People change. People grow.

I stand up, rather awkwardly. "I'm going to have to get back to work now," I say. John wasn't happy when I told him I had an emergency. He says he needs all hands on-deck, especially given I've got my usual afternoon off tomorrow and I'm taking the whole off Friday off too. "But we can talk properly later."

Sophie stands and gives me a hug—a hug that has my heart pounding and my head spinning. The scent of her perfume is intoxicating, and I don't want to let go. Because this just feels… right.

She pulls back a little, and her face is so close to mine.

And then I do it. I lean forward and press my lips to hers. Sophie trembles a little, but then she kisses me back, her lips soft and urgent.

Her hands tangle in my hair, and I press myself closer, kissing deeper and deeper.

Then I pull back. "Wow. Uh, I'm sorry, I—" I stop when I realize she's staring at me, and I can't quite work out whether she's happy or shocked or both.

Her expression is blank, the planes of her face smooth, giving nothing away.

"I've not kissed a girl before," she says.

"Woman," I correct automatically. It's one of my pet peeves really, women being called girls when we're not. But now probably isn't the time to criticize her. "Sorry."

And I stare at her, waiting for her to say something. But she doesn't.

Oh God. I read it wrong. Completely wrong. "I'm so sorry."

"It's…" Her voice is small. "It's okay. I… I just need. I don't know what I need."

"It's fine," I say. "I've got to go."

Sophie doesn't stop me as I leave. And I really want her to. I want her to shout my name as I head out, to cause one of those romantic scenes. But she doesn't. She does nothing.

Tears pierce the corners of my eyes. Sophie's inaction shouldn't sting this much. I know that. And I don't know why it does.

Dylan frowns at me over FaceTime the next day. "Don't tell me you're going to mope around the whole day?"

I shake my head and try to prop up my phone on my knees—but it just falls down. I retrieve it quickly and resign to the fact I'll just have to hold it. I'm sort of half curled up on the sofa, with my biggest woolly jumper on. It's like a tent on me, but it was my grandmother's, and I wear it when I need comfort. Work was torturous this morning, and I just need time to rest now. "I'm not moping."

Dylan makes a hooting sound as he laughs. "Seriously? You're got to get out and about. Don't stay cooped up."

I look out the window. "It's snowing again. It's too cold to go out."

"So, you're sitting there moping."

"I'm not moping!"

He sighs a really overexaggerated sigh. "You *so* are. Come on, Court, everyone gets rejected. It's part of life."

I wrinkle my nose.

"You've been rejected before, right?" he asks.

I shake my head. "No. And it bloody hurts." I've not had any romantic relationships before where I've been rejected—I mean, I've done the rejecting and the breaking up myself, but even those relationships were different. They weren't like this. They weren't like what me and Sophie have—and I know there's something here.

She just doesn't want to admit it. Is it because she doesn't want people to know she's bi—biromantic? I mean, she doesn't even know that I know that because she doesn't know she's been speaking to me on the helpline.

I take a shaky breath. Maybe it's better that nothing does happen between us—nothing more than already has, anyway—given what I know about her and what she doesn't know about me. I can hardly say, in a month's time or whatever, *Oh yeah, I forgot to say, but I'm Tabitha!*

"It's going to be so awkward seeing her again," I tell Dylan, thinking about later when we'll both be at Zara's. I've literally had no contact with Sophie since yesterday when I kissed her. I thought about calling in the evening—like I'd promised her we'd talk then, before I then ruined everything—but I just couldn't bring myself to start a call. "Like, ridiculously awkward."

"Then don't." His answer is simple.

I sigh. "But I have to—this stupid prank competition. We're both supposed to go over to Zara's later to find out the rules for the final round."

"Well, that'll be over soon. Then you'll never have to see her again."

"Only I will," I point out, "as she lives right here now. God, maybe I should move."

"Courtney." Dylan sounds exasperated. "You're not moving because of this. Don't be silly. Just chill, okay? Now, pull yourself together and snap out of it."

I narrow my eyes, but I don't know if he can see it on his screen. I don't like this assertive Dylan though, not when I just want to be left alone.

"Oh, for God's sake, Courtney. Do Kayla and I need to come 'round?"

"No!"

Dylan being here is the last thing I want—because I think I do just need to get this sadness out of system, that's all. I just want to have a good cry, and then I'll be fine.

He makes a noise deep in his throat. "Well, tell me how it's going at work then?"

"Work?" I frown. "But you hate me talking about that. You say it's boring."

"Well then tell me about it in an entertaining way. Describe all your colleagues as if they're dogs."

"Dogs?" The corners of my mouth twitch.

"Well, we need some entertainment," he says.

And with that, we begin trying to match dog breeds to each of my colleagues. And I suppose it does start to help me feel better.

Later that day, Sophie's already at Zara's when I arrive, and I try to act normally. Try to pretend that I didn't kiss her yesterday and that she didn't sort of reject me.

Zara talks energetically about the final round of Queen of Pranks, but refuses to tell us the current score. Zoe isn't here, and I can't work out if things are any better between the two twins. But I realize I haven't talked to Zoe in a few days—because I've been so wrapped up in my own drama.

I'm back to being a shitty friend. I make a mental note to call her later.

"The final will take place next week," Zara says. "So, you've got a week one and one day to make your plan. We'll do it Friday evening—so make sure you've got nothing else on then. It'll be filmed in both your apartments, so you may want to do a quick tidy up or something." Her eyes flit to me. "And you'll each have an hour to prepare something *in* the other's apartment. It's got to be the ultimate thing, okay? This is where you really show what you're made of. Each of you will have one of us with you, filming preparation in the apartments and then the other's reaction as they discover the prank. You've got until then to work out what exactly you want to do as the final prank."

"Can we use other people?" Sophie asks.

Zara shakes her head. "No. This has got to be a prank that doesn't rely on others being there, apart from whoever's filming, but we won't be able to do anything to help. And the prank has also got to be something that you leave in place at the apartment."

I frown. "Like a booby trap?"

"Exactly!" Zara says. "But nothing dangerous. And you'll have to be creative," Zara adds.

I nod, but I'm not invested in the pranks any more. Not when more serious stuff is going on with Sophie. I mean, have I ruined everything?

It seems to take forever before I can make my escape from Zara's, and when I do, Sophie doesn't leave with me. I mean, why would she? I've probably made her so uncomfortable that she's choosing to go back to Mrs. Dalton's, despite everything that has happened there, than go back to mine.

I could kick myself.

As I walk back, I phone Zoe—and I feel bad that maybe I'm wanting to talk about Zoe's health to distract me, because I shouldn't be using my friend like that. But she doesn't pick up, and I'm back to wallowing in my sadness about Sophie.

THIRTY-THREE

Sophie

VICTORIA'S NOT HOME, and I've never been so glad to walk into an empty apartment. We've still not talked since I walked out of that doctor's office, and it's like walking on eggshells around her. This morning, she just watched me at breakfast, and sniffed every now and again, looking hurt. I could feel all the anger simmering away inside her, and I can't help but wonder when she's going to explode.

On my bed, I scroll to the chat window with Courtney. I stare at the memes we'd sent each other. I think of how happy I feel every time her name lights up my phone.

And she kissed me. She *likes* me.

Just as I like her. And I think about that kiss—and then how I just let her walk away. God, why didn't I say anything? Or do anything? I just watched her walk away, my eyes on the cartoon bumble bee tattoo on the back of her neck, watching it get smaller and smaller with distance. And I didn't even speak to her at Zara's. I just sort of pretended that she wasn't there. Oh God.

I type out a new message: *I like you too.*

Then I press send before I can chicken out.

Immediately, nervous energy fills me and I feel sick. What if she didn't really mean to kiss me? What if—

No. Don't start thinking like that, I warn myself. I've done all I can now. Haven't I?

But I'm staring at the phone, waiting for a reply. I mean, it's not that late. Only half eight, so she won't have gone to bed, and before when we were sending those memes to each other, that was this time.

I try not to picture her downstairs. Is she sitting with her phone? Or watching a film or something without her phone nearby, stroking Sergeant—who is definitely not in this apartment again—trying to distract herself? Because she'll need distracting, I'm sure. I saw how down she looked at Zara's earlier. She barely even spoke, and when she did, her voice was just flat.

A key turning in the lock of the front door makes me jump. Oh God. Victoria's back?

I tiptoe to the edge of my room and open the door a crack. It's Martin. I breathe a sigh of relief as he stomps by. He doesn't look toward me or my door, just goes straight to his room. Reeks of cigarette smoke though. That and something else that I can't identify.

When Victoria eventually gets in, an hour later, I hear her pacing the corridor outside my room. Hear her steps on the creaking floor. She's still wearing her shoes, and I know that's going to be annoying Courtney downstairs.

Courtney. No. I'm not thinking about her. She hasn't replied which means I've blown it.

I wait and wait for Victoria to knock on my door or something. Wait and wait and wait. But there's nothing. Just the pacing continuing, before I hear her in the bathroom, running the bath.

Maybe she thinks it's too late to say anything now. Maybe I'll have that joy at breakfast. Because she's going to say *something* at some point. And I'm dreading that conversation.

THIRTY-FOUR

Courtney

FOR A SECOND, when I see Sophie's message the next morning when I finally plug in my phone to the mains, I think I must be dreaming. Must still be asleep. But I pinch myself—actually do the cliché to check—and wow, it hurts so I guess I am awake. A grin spreads across my face as I stare at the words.

I like you too.

She likes me!

I feel giddy with sudden energy, and I leap out of my chair and run out of my apartment and up to hers.

She answers the door immediately.

"Hey," I say to Sophie, and this feels weird. Am I supposed to hold her hand or what? Kiss? I mean, we've both admitted we like each other, but what do we do now?

"Do you want to go out anywhere?" I ask. "Like, for breakfast?"

Sophie nods. "Anything to get away from Victoria."

My eyes widen. "What's happened?"

"Nothing so far. She's just simmering away. Half the time she seems angry, half the time disappointed. But she's going to have it out with me at some point. I know that. But she's still in bed now."

I nod, and then Sophie's grabbing her coat. She locks the front door of the Daltons' apartment and checks it three times. We stop at mine so I can get my thicker coat too—it's even colder this morning—then we head out to the local coffee shop.

"We'll have to make sure Zara doesn't find out about this," Sophie says.

"Why?" I frown.

"Else she'd insist on filming it, I'm sure. And I'm not sure she's going to like it if she finds out we're...whatever we are. It doesn't exactly go hand-in-hand with the prank show."

A smile slips across my face. *Whatever we are.* So, Sophie wants it to be something. A warm glow fills me.

"So, what's something that you don't like?" Sophie asks me as we eat croissants and coffee. Or rather, I'm eating mine, she's just nibbling at hers.

The café's really busy, and there was only one small sofa free, so of course we're squashed together on this, with our trays on a really low coffee table that means we have to lean down and bend forward a lot to reach the items. There are also two small toddlers screaming at each other right behind us. It's honestly ear-piercing.

"Something I don't like? Well, that cat of yours for a start. He's always in my apartment."

She laughs softly. "You like him really."

I snort. "Nah. Anyway, what is up with his name? Sergeant *Ginger Paws*? He's completely white."

Her laugh gets stronger. "Martin named him—he and Victoria got him as a kitten. They'd visited the litter shortly after the kittens were born, and picked out the one they wanted. A white cat with ginger paws. Reserved him. But when they came to collect him when he was old enough, they found he'd transformed into a different cat."

"What?" I frown.

"Apparently, the owners tried to tell them that he'd never had ginger paws, that it was the same kitten, when it really wasn't. Martin was only little then, like six or something, and he'd named the other kitten. He was upset at first, but they got Sergeant, and well, Martin really wanted that name, so they didn't change it."

I nod. "Right. Okay."

"Anyway—something you don't like?" Sophie prompts again.

I shrug. "Well, whatever's set those two off." I indicate the two screaming toddlers.

"They're fighting over the Hello Kitty toy," Sophie says.

"They are?"

She nods, and then tucks a strand of her hair behind her ear.

"Well, I don't like Hello Kitty then," I grumble. I rub my forehead—forgetting I've got greasy croissant fingers and wince as I feel the grease on my forehead. I grab a napkin and wipe it off, trying to ignore the amused look on Courtney's face. "Don't laugh," I tell her.

"Wouldn't dream of it," she says.

She's so close I can feel her body heat. We draped our coats on the back of the sofa when we sat, and it's got those really springy, soft cushions that try to swallow you. Sophie and I keep sliding farther down in the seats—and closer together—

and I want to just put my arms around her, hug her, kiss her, but I also don't want to scare her away.

"Well, one thing I don't like is spiders," she says.

I crack a smile. "I remember that."

"You do?"

I nod. "At St. Bridget's—I remember you freaking out completely because there was one in your room or something."

Her face reddens. "I didn't make a massive thing of it, though."

"You had the maintenance guy called out especially."

She laughs. "It still wasn't that big a thing though."

I raise my eyebrows. "We had an assembly the next day about what the emergency telephones in our rooms are for."

"Well, if they didn't want us calling maintenance, perhaps they shouldn't have printed the extension numbers by our phones." She laughs, and her whole face lights up. "But those phones were awful, right?"

I nod. I only had to use one once when Zoe had been in the shower. Zara and I had heard this almighty crash from in there, but Zoe had locked the door. We couldn't get in to see if she was all right, and she wasn't answering our shouts through the door. Miss Aylott and the dorm receptionist had come rushing up with master keys. We'd found Zoe unconscious in the shower, and for ages after that Zoe had been afraid of the shower, convinced she had a brain injury from it, despite doctors checking her over, and she always made sure never to lock the door after that.

Sophie pulls a flake of pastry off her croissant and presses it onto the little plate that's on her lap then tries to smear the pastry around. It doesn't really work.

She looks up at me, realizes that I'm watching her do this. "Oh," she says.

"What?"

"I... I haven't told you. But I've got, uh, issues with food."

"With food?" My voice sounds strange, flat.

"I've been having therapy for it," she says. "I just find it hard to eat things that aren't on my meal plan—and it should've been cereal and fruit today." She laughs but it's too high-pitched. Anyway, do you remember that book we had in year seven?" Sophie asks me. She puts her croissant down and delicately licks her fingers.

"Book?" I ask.

"Notebook. Where we kept track of the points we gave each other."

Oh. That. That was when we were on much friendlier terms than at any other point in our school days. Each week, we decided between the two of us who was victorious, and we get a running scoreboard.

"I found it," Sophie says. "When I was clearing my stuff out from the London flat. It..." She glances at me. "It made me smile. I've got it at Victoria's now."

Just the mention of that woman's name makes the air suddenly seem cold. The chat and chaos around us seems to fade, even though I know it's not.

"What are you going to do about her?" I ask Sophie. "You can still stay at mine, you know, if you want to. If that would be easier."

"Thanks," she says. "But I need to sort things out with her. She is my family."

"Just...just don't let her make you think what we are is bad or anything," I say.

Sophie nods. "She needs re-educating." A slight frown crosses her face. "There's this helpline I've been calling—you know, specifically about being ace—and I wonder if they'd speak to her?"

I nearly stop breathing. The helpline? She's bringing this up now? I take a deep breath.

"Maybe I can persuade Victoria to be a bit more open to the idea?" She shrugs, and then picks up her croissant again.

"Maybe," I say. "But do you want me to be there when you discuss this with her? Like, we could do it in-person?" Alarm bells are ringing in my ears. I'm working at the center tonight. Sophie may not have recognized who 'Tabitha' sounds like, but if I end up speaking to Mrs. Dalton on the line too, I can't help but think that'll be pushing my luck.

"It's okay," Sophie says. "There's a great woman at the helpline. I'm sure she'll be happy to help. Anyway, I don't want to put anything on your plate. You're busy enough with work."

"Right," I say, and I try to swallow down the lump in my throat. Try to pretend that everything is normal. My stomach feels queasy though as I watch Sophie play some more with her croissant. She is deconstructing it, one piece of flaky pastry at a time. And I can't help but think that that's what's happening to me. Sooner or later, my layers—my secrets—are going to be stripped away, and then she'll know what I know and what I've done.

THIRTY-FIVE

Courtney

I'M A BALL of nerves for the rest of the day, and I call Peter twice, ready to ask if I can swap shifts with him, but then each time his phone goes onto answerphone and something stops me from leaving a message. Because what if Mrs. Mitchell then looks into why I want to swap? Sure, I do the day-to-day running of the helpline, but she still oversees it all.

"It'll be fine, won't it?" I say to Sergeant Ginger Paws who's in my apartment again. He's stretched out on the welcome mat, carefully licking one of his arms.

Sergeant Ginger Paws doesn't do a great job of reassuring me.

Right. I need a plan. I need a plan for tonight when Sophie and Mrs. Dalton are on the line. I take a deep breath. Is there some way I can distort my voice?

Or maybe I should just come clean to Sophie? Maybe—

The clock strikes four, and I look at the clock-face. Two hours until my shift at the center starts.

I begin placing my apartment, walking round and round, and Sergeant Ginger Paws's eyes follow me. I pull out my phone and text Zoe, asking her how she is.

Someone knocks at my door, and I nearly jump a foot in the air.

My heart pounds as I rush toward it. Sergeant Ginger Paws gets up slowly and lazily, and then mews at the door before he turns on his heel and walks over to the kitchen.

I pull the door open. Two men stand there, both wearing overalls.

"Here to replace your washer," one of them says.

"Washer? The washing machine?" I stare at them, bewildered.

"Yep." One of them checks some papers on a clipboard. "And we're taking the other one away."

My head spins. Is this Dylan? Did he order it? He kept saying I should get a new one, and I probably annoyed him enough by complaining to him about it, and then asking him and Jack to help 'fix' the old one.

"Uh, can I see some ID?" I ask the man.

He takes a card out of his pocket. It's for the appliances shop in town. "Want to phone them to check?"

He sounds annoyed though, so I shake my head, feeling all flustered.

Time seems to speed up way too fast, and then the men are taking away my washing machine. Water's somehow still dripping from it.

A few minutes pass, and then they're back, lifting a large pink washing machine.

I stare at the Hello Kitty washing machine. My heart pounds.

"Is it...it's not a toy, is it?" My voice wavers. I don't know whether to laugh or not—only this can't be a prank, because the final week's pranks are taking place during designated hours. But still, I'm looking for hidden cameras or something.

"Of course it's not a toy!" One of the men laughs. "Fully functioning washer, this!"

I nod, the corners of my mouth twitching into a smile.

Sophie—this has to be down to her. I text her quickly, thanking her and tell her I love the joke. She replies with a smiley face and then a laughing emoji, and I'm left staring at the Hello Kitty washing machine. Just how the hell did Sophie arrange it all so quickly?

"So, what's the problem?" Mum says. Her voice is tinny on the phone. It often is, and it must be because she still uses that ancient landline. "You needed a new washing machine, and now you've got one."

"But it's Hello Kitty." I mean, that in and of itself should say enough.

"So? No one's going to see it. And if it's a fully functioning machine, then you've got no problem."

"Well, I suppose," I say. I glance at the machine. It's got half an hour left of its cleaning cycle. The manual said to run it on the hottest cotton cycle before its first use "But what about when people come around?"

And—oh my God. The final prank—Sophie's taking over my apartment for an hour next Friday to set up her final prank on me. The washing machine's going to be in all the shots, I'm sure of it. Can I hide it with a sheet or something?

"Don't be so silly," Mum says. "And don't worry constantly about what people think. It's nice of your friend to get it for you."

"Mmhmm." I swallow hard. Mum thinks Dylan got it for me as a jokey-but-serious present. Something stopped me from telling her that I suspect Sophie is behind it—because Mum doesn't know about Sophie and me. And I hate that I haven't told her, but I just worry that she's not going to get it.

I think it'll be better to tell her about me and Sophie in-person, which means I'll have to take the train up to her house soon.

"I mean, if someone wants to buy me a fancy new washing machine, I'd be very happy," she says. "It's just like what Glynis from the Tai Chi group is always saying: *Be grateful for what you have.* And you, Courtney Davenport, you've got great friends. Really good friends."

Good friends—and I have. Dylan and the twins. And now Sophie. Well, until the call tonight at the center—because I just know it's all going to unravel. It's like I've got a sixth sense for it.

As Mum and I talk, chatting pretty much about nothing now, I watch the countdown on the washing machine's screen. When it gets to zero, it'll also be time for me to leave.

I've never not wanted to go to the center and talk on the Places for Aces helpline before. But now I'm a bag of nerves, and I keep telling myself not to be. Maybe—just maybe—whoever else is volunteering there tonight will answer the phone when Sophie phones?

THIRTY-SIX

Sophie

VICTORIA IS STAYING out of my way—that much, I am sure about. I stay all day at home, and she's out for all of it. At one point, she texts me to tell me she's seeing friends tonight. But that's all the message says. No *how are you?* No *there's food in the fridge*. All friendliness has gone.

I take a deep breath. I think this might even be worse than just having her have a go at me—because this is dragging me out. Even though I'm the only one in the apartment, the atmosphere is awful. The air feels too thick, like I'm going to choke on it.

Once six o'clock comes around, I grab my phone and dial the Places for Aces number—but I stop short of pressing the call button. I stare at the area code and frown. How didn't I realize it before? It's the same area code as Victoria's landline.

Places for Aces is based around here?

I open the browser on my phone and google the charity. Sure enough, it's near here—in Exeter. My heart pounds. What are the odds of that happening? I take a deep breath. There's an address listed on the website, and I take a screenshot of it.

Tabitha has helped me so much, and although we're not talking as regularly now, I feel like I owe her a thank you at the very least. But I also need her help with the step-mother situation. And in-person may be easier.

I frown. Would she mind if I turned up at the center? I mean, I think about Victoria and how she always prefers in-person appointments to telephone calls. She says it's more personal—and maybe if I can arrange an in-person session for Victoria and I to attend with Tabitha, I'll get more of the result I'm hoping for? That's if Tabitha is happy to do this.

I mean, I should probably meet Tabitha in person tonight anyway, first, before I go with Victoria.

I take a deep breath and then grab my coat.

I'll get there in no time.

I didn't think it was possible, but it's got even colder tonight. No new snow is falling, but the pavements are icy. The sky is dark, and everything just *feels* cold. By the time I get to the building that I think is Places for Aces, my feet are numb and I'm sure the tip of nose has gone bright red.

I push open the door, and am immediately engulfed by a bout of hot air. It's welcoming, to say the least.

I listen for a moment, staring around the empty foyer. I can hear someone talking, and there are two doors leading off to the left and the right respectively. The voice appears to be floating through from the left, so carefully I push that door open and—

Courtney. My eyes widen as I spot her. She's not facing me—her dark hair is tied back, but I can see the tattoo on her neck. The bumble bees. It's her.

She volunteers here too?

The phone on her desk rings, and she answers it. "Hello, this is the Places for Aces helpline," Courtney says, but her voice is shaking. She's nervous? I frown. Is this her first day here? Maybe she'd been thinking about doing this, and then I mentioned this place to her. "M-m-my name is Tabitha. How may I help you?"

Tabitha? Why would she use that name? Why—

Everything inside me drops away.

I make a choking sound, and my eyes widen, and, suddenly, it's too hot in here. There's a rushing sound in my ears.

Courtney is still talking—but I can't make out her words now. It's all just background noise, *all* of it.

She is Tabitha. She's the one who's been talking to me.

Nausea twists my stomach into knots. Courtney… Tabitha…

No!

I take a deep breath that rasps against the inside of my throat. All this time, she's known and she's *pretended*. Courtney—Courtney who I *like*.

I back away and—

Thud.

I crash into the door, and the sound is enough to make Courtney turn. Her expression slackens as she sees me. She nearly drops the phone, and I stare at her, frozen.

"I… You knew all this time?" I hiss. "You pretended and…that's messed up, Courtney. That's—" I can't even think of the words I need. Can't even sort out my scrambled brain. So many thoughts are flying around, and I can't make sense of all this. "I thought I knew you…"

"You do," Courtney or Tabitha or whoever she is whispers.

"You... You *catfished* me… You—"

"No, it wasn't like that. I—"

But I don't listen to her. I just turn and run.

THIRTY-SEVEN

Courtney

THIS CAN'T BE happening. It actually can't! I was going to tell Sophie, of course I was. I wasn't going to keep it from her forever, especially if the two of us do seem to be going somewhere, but she wasn't supposed to find out like this. No, this is the worst way she could've found out.

I stare at the door—even though Sophie left through it ages ago. I can't even tell exactly how long has passed. I've just been staring at the door, letting the phone ring and ring and ring.

I'm the only one in here. No others tonight, it's just me—because Tammy called in sick, and I only found out when I got here.

But I… I should go after Sophie. I know that.

I stand up, but just doing so seems to make the phone ring even louder.

I flinch. I should answer it.

But what about Sophie?

Steeling myself, I answer the phone. "Places for Aces. Tabitha speaking. How may I help you?" I say the words too quickly, and they seem to end up bouncing against each other.

The caller—a man, I think—starts speaking, but I can't focus on his words. All I can think is that Sophie's out there. That she's upset, that she thinks I catfished her, betrayed her—and I did. I should've been honest. Why the hell didn't I tell her as soon as I realized?

I feel sick, and now there's a caller on the line. A man expecting me to help and listen, but I have no idea what he's just said.

"I'm so sorry, can you repeat that?" I say. "The line's bad, and I didn't quite catch it."

The man sighs, sounds exasperated, but he repeats it. He wants to know the difference between aro and ace. I rattle off the answers, but I've never felt so disconnected to my work, and I know this isn't good. He should have my full attention, but he hasn't.

Sophie has. But I can't leave. I have to stay. I have to help people, even if I've just hurt the one person I most want to help.

The moment the shift's over, I lock up in record time and head back. My heart pounds all the way home, and twice I dry-retch. People give me odd looks, probably think I'm on drugs or something.

I go straight to Sophie's apartment, but Mrs. Dalton answers the door.

"Uh, is Sophie there?"

Mrs. Dalton glares at me. "You're the one who's put all this nonsense into her head, telling her she's asexual." She spits the word at me like it's poison. "And pretending to be someone else. It's disgusting behavior. Absolutely disgusting."

"No," I try to say, but she cuts me off, has another go at me, and I can't help but wonder what exactly Sophie has said to her. I mean, it sounds like Sophie's blamed the whole ace thing on me, saying that I persuaded her she was like this?

Once Mrs. Dalton has finished chewing me up and spitting me out, I call out to Sophie—because she's got to be in there, right?

"I'm so sorry," I shout, and then Mrs. Dalton slams the door in my face.

I retreat back downstairs, shaking. Oh God. How has it come to this?

I messed up. Big time. And now Sophie hates me, and she has every right to. I should've been honest with her. Mrs. Mitchell always said if anyone we know in real life phones the helpline then we shouldn't continue with them, but transfer them.

But I didn't.

And now it's all snowballed, and Sophie knows and hates me.

Oh God. I put my head in my hands and cry and cry and cry.

THIRTY-EIGHT

Sophie

"HAS SHE GONE?" I ask, peering around the doorway to my room.

"Yes," Victoria says. She moves away from the door and glances at me, a look of pure sympathy on her face. "Look, honey, there must be something wrong with that girl. Or she's mixed up in something dangerous. Maybe this is a cult, and she was trying to recruit you? But it's a good job you found out now before you became proper friends."

Found out now. I take a deep breath and wonder what she'd say if she really knew how I felt about Courtney. How I want to see her all the time. How amazing it felt when we kissed.

I almost can't believe this has happened—it doesn't feel real. I'm just…numb.

"I think we'd better call the police," she says. "We've no idea how big this cult is. We should let all the neighbors know, too. We could all be in danger."

"Victoria, *please*." I breathe deeply, trying to keep calm. "It's not a cult."

"It certainly sounds like one—she lured you in, becoming your friend and pretending to be someone else on the phone."

"I don't want to talk about it," I snap. My heart pounds, and I feel guilty that I've turned all this on Courtney like this, and that I've even been agreeing with Victoria about asexuality being something that needs fixing. Because I'm betraying myself now, and Courtney and everyone else who's ace, but I just don't know what to do. At least Courtney's getting the full wrath of my step-mother's fury now, because if I had Victoria going on at *me* about how unnatural asexuality is, I don't think I could cope. I need Victoria to be on my side now. I need kind words. I need some sort of sympathy for everything that's happened. I need to be held and looked after.

And I never thought Courtney would betray me.

But, then again, I betrayed her at school. Is this revenge?

No. She wouldn't do that. Would she?

I shake my head. I feel like screaming.

"Let's have a quiet night in," Victoria says. "We can watch a film. You can choose it. I'll get some popcorn."

And with that she bumbles off to the kitchen, still muttering under her breath about Courtney. Fresh tears fall down my face as I realize Victoria's most definitely going to talk to the neighbors tomorrow. She'll be outing Courtney, just as Janey did at school.

And, again, it's my fault.

I get ready to say something when Victoria brings the popcorn in here. To try and correct what I've said, what she thinks—only... Only I'm scared and I can't.

So, I'm silent and we watch the film, and I don't think I've ever felt so awful.

THIRTY-NINE

Courtney

THE WEEKEND AND Monday pass in a numb blur where I don't speak to anyone and ignore all calls from the twins and Dylan. I send Sophie texts saying how sorry I am, but they remain unanswered. I call a few times, leave on voicemail message, and then I stop—I get the message: she doesn't want to speak to me at all.

On Tuesday I go through the motions of the day at work, but I barely take anything in. I make stupid mistakes on drawings and then forget all the feedback my colleagues give me. I just can't concentrate.

Sally tries to talk to me, tries to get me to open up, but I just can't bring myself to say anything. I just feel sick and empty. My stomach churns. I haven't eaten all day. I can't.

Just as I'm about to leave the office—eight agonizingly slow hours later—my phone rings. I snatch it up, part of me convinced it's going to be Sophie. That she's ready to talk, that she's realized there must be an explanation of some sorts.

But it's not her. It's Mrs. Mitchell.

"Hello, Courtney," she says, her voice smooth and slow—but that tone makes my heart sink. She normally sounds upbeat, and I know now that this is not going to be an upbeat conversation. "I'm afraid we've had a complaint about you."

"A complaint?"

"A family member of one of the callers who's spoken regularly to you has complained," she says. "They were very acephobic and, normally, I wouldn't really take what they say seriously—only she did mention something of great concern."

I tremble.

"I then spoke to the individual involved in this—Sophie Sway. She claims to know you from school, and that you've been talking to her, posing at Tabitha, while *also* being involved with her in a relationship?"

I shove my free hand through my hair, pushing it away from my face, and then I take a deep breath. "We only got together recently—like I don't know if you can even call it anything?"

"But you'd still been talking to her for a while?" The line crackles.

"Yes." My legs start to shake.

"And you knew from the start that this was her? Someone that you knew in real life?"

Shame fills me. "Yes."

"And you did not declare that to me."

"No. I didn't. I…" I want to scream. "I should've—I know that…and…" I can't even speak. My tears are falling too fast, and everyone who's still in the office is looking at me.

"Okay," Mrs. Mitchell says. "I need to do some investigating into this. It's a very serious matter, as I'm sure you can understand. And, in the meantime, it's best if you take a break from the helpline."

A break? My chest drops. I love my job there. I love helping people.

But I know Mrs. Mitchell is right. It's all my fault. I messed up. I wasn't honest. And look where it's got me.

The next two days also pass in a blur. I can't think or concentrate on anything. I call in sick to work both days—and it's enough for Sally to make a visit to my apartment after work on Thursday. She calls through the letterbox, tells me it's her, but I don't move from where I've cocooned myself on the sofa. I don't answer the door.

I don't want to speak to anyone.

Dylan's video calls remain unanswered. As do Zara's and Zoe's calls.

It's a good job my mum doesn't call, because I'd never not answer her, and then I'd end up telling her everything—and I just can't cope with getting into it all with someone now.

I just want to wrap myself up in my own world and pretend none of it happened.

Someone bangs at my door. Then Zara's shrill voice calls through, demands that I open the door else she'll kick it down.

And it's only because I half believe her that I do get up and open it.

She waltzes straight in. Zoe follows her.

"Right, what the hell has been going on?" Zara demands. "You've not been online at all and we were worried, and Dylan was saying it was something to do with Sophie, but that we should talk to you. And then we came around here, and your neighbor's just been spouting all sorts about you down by the entrance to Hawklands."

"What?" I stare at her.

Zoe shuts the door carefully behind her and then moves farther into my apartment, standing next to Zara.

"She was saying you're in a cult." Zara snorts. "Saying that you're trying to convert everyone into being ace. I mean, we told them what a load of bullshit that was—and how acephobic that was, and now they think we're members of it too."

My heart sinks. Sophie must've used me as a scapegoat. And, really, I can't blame her—but I'm worried what hearing all the acephobic rubbish is going to be doing to her, knowing she's ace too.

"So, spill," Zara says. "Because we've missed out on the drama of the century, by the looks of it, and I'm not happy about that."

I don't want to talk about it, but of course Zara drags it out of me. Everything about Sophie and me getting together (Zara gasps), everything about speaking to Sophie on the helpline (Zara's eyes widen), and everything about the call with Mrs. Mitchell (Zara looks sad). Zara then calls Mrs. Dalton several choice names, before she wraps me up in a hug at the end.

"You can't tell anyone Sophie's ace though," I say. "I mean, I shouldn't have said that to you."

Zoe sits on the arm of the sofa and gives me a sympathetic look. "We won't."

"She's a right traitor though," Zara says. "She's ace and she's allowing her step-mother to say all that about asexuality—and you." She shakes her head. "But don't worry. We'll get our own back on Sophie in the final round of Queen of Pranks."

I groan. "Please—I can't do that show anymore. Not with her."

"But, Courtney. We've got to film the last bit—and I'm sure Sophie is going to move away. Probably Mrs. Dalton too. She's not going to want to live next to a cult, is she?" She laughs.

I do not laugh and look to Zoe for help. .

"Maybe you should just use the film you've already got for it," Zoe suggests, reaching out and patting my arm.

"We need the final round," Zara says. "But I'm sure as hell going to have words with Sophie about all of this."

"No, please don't," I say. "I don't want Sophie hating me even more than she already does."

"But she's spreading rumours about you."

"It's Mrs. Dalton, not her."

"But she's allowing it! Courtney, Sophie's not innocent in all this."

"Compared to me, she is," I say. "What I did was unethical. I deserve all this."

"No, you don't," Zoe says. She stands up. "I think we need to get you out of here, just for a bit."

I look at her properly and notice the dark circles under her eyes—darker than last time I saw her. And of course I think of her diagnosis and realize *again* what a shitty friend I've been to her.

"I don't want to go anywhere," I whisper.

"Nonsense," Zara says, linking arms me. "You're coming with us. Now."

"Chin up," Dylan says.

"Chin up," Kayla says.

"Chin up," the twins say, and then everyone laughs apart from me.

We're at Dylan's house, and it's nearly Kayla's bed time, but she's showing everyone how wide awake she is. First, she was showing me her karaoke machine, and then her collection of teddy bears. Now she's telling me 'chin up' over and over again. Brilliant.

I just want to go home. My heart isn't in this get-together.

Eventually, Dylan persuades Kayla to go to bed—so long as Zoe, who's her favorite, tells her a story about dragons. Zoe obliges, and an hour later, it's just us adults up. There's a film on, but I'm just staring at it glassily.

Zoe keeps glancing at me during the film—I think she's checking I'm not crying or something.

When the ending credits roll, I'm relieved.

I just want to get out of here.

"Don't forget to come up with an idea for your prank tomorrow," Zara says. "Because I'm guessing you haven't already?"

"*Tomorrow?*" I stare at her.

"Uh, yeah, that's always been the plan. Final filming is tomorrow. We've got the grand pranks, and then I need to do several interview clips with you."

I groan. So that means seeing Sophie tomorrow.

Wonderful.

FORTY

Courtney

"THIS IS IT, the final round of Queen of Pranks," Zara says, pointing the camera at me. "So, you better make it a good one. You've got an hour each to prepare the final prank in the other's apartment."

We're in the corridor outside the Daltons' apartment. Just me and Zara. Sophie's downstairs with Zara.

"Oh, I will," I say, adjusting the weight of my rucksack. I know I've got to use this hour wisely. I need Sophie to know how sorry I am. It's my only chance. She's not been returning my calls or answering my messages. To be honest, I'm surprised she's still here and still taking part in the game at all.

The door to the Dalton's apartment is unlocked, and with a shaking hand, I open it. I wonder what Mrs. Dalton would say if she knew I was here or what Zoe and Zara said to her to get her and Martin to vacate the house.

In the kitchen, I slip the rucksack off and haul it up and onto the table. I open it. Inside are one hundred photos of me—each one photoshopped with a bubble coming out of my head. It's supposed to be one of those speech-bubbles, but it looks weird. The text inside the bubbles ranges from apologies to the various things I like about Sophie. I sorted it all out last night, and then drove to the office to use their printers. I'll square it with John later.

I grab the giant roll of tape from my bag and stick the images all over her house. Zara follows me with the camera for the first ten minutes, but then I think she gets bored. It's not exactly exciting stuff. In fact, it's a bit disconcerting really, having so many of me watching me. But as I finish the kitchen and move onto the living room, I wonder if I've made a huge mistake. Maybe my face is the last thing Sophie will want to look at.

But I have to try.

"Time," Zara calls. She's outside in the hallway now, and for a moment, I don't think that an hour really can have passed. But looking at the clock tells me that it has.

I join her outside the apartment, in the foyer.

"I'm staying here to film Sophie's reaction upon entering, and Zoe's downstairs, ready to film you." Zara gives me an encouraging smile. "So, everything's ready in there?"

I nod. When she heard about my plan, very late last night, she seemed a little disappointed—it wasn't the exciting, grand prank she'd been anticipating. But she didn't try and get me to change it, and I think she realizes now how much Sophie does mean to me. After all, she's never seen me this upset.

"Good. Then you go to your apartment, and I'll wait for Sophie to get here."

In the stairwell, I pass Sophie. She gives me a sheepish nod. I note that she's holding several tote bags, all of which seem to be empty. I wonder what she's done to my flat. And really, this prank's going to be worse than any of hers so far. So much worse. I know that. She's not going to care about hurting me now, not when I've betrayed her like this. And sure—all the cult stuff that she must've told Mrs. Dalton hurt me, but I know I'm the one in the wrong here.

I open the door of my apartment, cringing, waiting for a bucket of water to fall on my head or something. Or flour.

But it doesn't. Nothing falls.

I step into the kitchen and—

Sergeant Ginger Paws stares back at me—from hundreds of places in the room.

I clap a hand to my mouth. She's done the same thing as me? Plastered photos up. Hers haven't got speech-bubbles photoshopped onto them—but still.

It feels a bit flat really, for the final of Zara's show. I can't help but think she's not going to be happy.

"This is amazing," Zoe says, speaking to the camera. "We don't even have to fake anything in editing—what a coincidence that they've both chosen a variation of the same prank." It sounds like the most unlikely thing for her to say— something much more suited to her sister—so I wonder if Zara's texted her that line. Especially as I don't think Zoe's ever spoken directly to the camera before. Plus, I know Zoe, and I bet she's thinking that this isn't really a prank.

"I wonder what Sophie thinks of it," I say.

I wonder if she's forgiven me.

I wonder if she can look me in the eye.

I wonder if there's any chance for us or if I really have blown things.

But I can't say those things—not on camera. Not when—

Something crashes above me.

I look up.

"What was that?" Zoe is all wide-eyed.

Then we hear screams.

My heart pounds. *Sophie.*

I turn fast, skidding on the tiled floor, and head for the door.

Sophie is still screaming.

My stomach twists as I head for the stairs. My breaths are ragged. There's a rushing sound filling my ears as I take the stairs two at a time.

"Sophie?" I shout. My heart pounds faster, harder. Nausea washes over me, and I force myself to speed up even more.

I throw open the door of her apartment and—

"Get away from her," I scream as I see the man towering over Sophie. She's on the floor, and he's holding a baseball bat.

FORTY-ONE

Sophie

"READY?" ZARA ASKS me, smiling.

She's got the camera way too close to my face and I've got no makeup on for once. My face feels naked, but I just didn't have the heart to make an effort. Not when I just want this to be over with.

I nod and open the door and—

Courtney's face stares at me from all around the hall.

Wonderful.

Everywhere I look, she's there.

Zara's smirking as she pans the camera round. Behind her, the door closes with a soft thud.

I rip the nearest poster off the wall, stare at the words. *I think you're amazing.* I take in the other phrases nearby. *I'm so sorry. I like how organized you are. I think you're going to be a bestselling author. I like your smile. Your eyes light up when you're happy. I miss you.*

"Well?" Zara prompts, thrusting the camera back toward me. The lens sticks out so far I have to step backward and—

The door flies open, and I brace myself to see Courtney, to get ready to talk to her, even though I don't want to.

But it isn't Courtney.

My hands turn to ice. The poster flutters to the ground. My stomach twists. My knees weaken as I stare at him. He's here—he can't be here! But he is.

Adam.

He's standing right there, in the doorway. A muscle in his jaw is pulsing, and he's breathing hard. He's also holding a baseball bat.

"Who the hell are you?" Zara turns, frowning.

Adam looks at her then ploughs toward me.

I shoot backward, into the living room, and trip over the coffee table. I fall, crashing onto the floor. Pain shoots through my right leg, and something in my chest tightens.

"Sophie!" Zara shrieks, but I can't see her.

I can only see him, and I'm screaming.

"Shut up!" Adam stops a few feet away, eyes widening as he takes in the surroundings. "Who's this?" He points at the poster of Courtney. "What the—" He reads a poster that says *I really like you.* "You've been cheating on me?"

"Uh, excuse me?" Zara shouts, and I see her behind Adam. "Get *out.*" She points at the door with the camera.

Adam laughs. "Who's this? Another girlfriend?"

"Zara, get help!" I try to crawl backward as Adam advances on me.

"No, you're staying here," Adam shouts, but I can't tell which of us he means. His eyes are on me, but he waves the bat in Zara's direction.

My heart pounds. He's not going to hurt me, is he? Or Zara? I mean, he wouldn't… Would he?

Menace fills Adam's eyes.

"Please, just go," I whisper.

"Go? Why would I ever want to go?" He laughs and his laugh is like a cockroach, crawling all over me.

I take a deep breath and then I scream again. I scream as loudly as I can. Someone has to hear me and call the police.

"I told you I'd find you!" Adam snarls. He shifts the weight of the baseball bat and edges nearer still and—

"Get away from her!" a voice shouts—*Courtney*.

I jolt, and then she's here, pulling Adam back. He swings the baseball bat around and there's a thud as it connects with something.

"I'm calling the police!" Zoe's voice. But I can't see her. "I'm—"

Adam swings the bat toward me, and I scramble to the right, away from him. Courtney's by my side, suddenly, pulling me along. Adrenaline pounds through me.

Zara shouts something and—

Zoe leaps at him. She grabs the bat, wrenches it from him, and holds it up, menacingly. "Get out," she shouts.

Adam laughs. "You wouldn't use that against me. Women don't know—"

She lunges at him, catching him in the ribs.

Adam screams as he staggers backward. "You little—"

"*Go.*" Zoe yells the word so loudly I jump. "Leave now."

Adam turns and looks at me. "I'll be back."

"No, you won't," Zoe says.

Adam snorts and then he looks toward the door. No one else is there. Courtney, Zara, and I are in the corner of the room. Zoe's the nearest one to him. He has a clean path to the exit.

He runs out of the living room, then out of the apartment.

"Oh my God." Zoe's voice is small, and she drops the bat. It clatters to the floor, catching the edge of the glass-topped coffee table as it goes. Her eyes are wide, and she's breathing hard.

"Wow," Zara says.

"Are you okay?" Courtney turns to me.

I nod, adrenaline still racing through my system. I can't stop staring at her. At how her nostrils are flaring because she's angry. How bright her eyes look. How she ran straight in here. Zoe, too.

"We need to call the police," Zoe says. "That's your ex? You need a restraining order."

"A restraining order?" I repeat, weakly.

Zoe nods, and then she's taking charge—and she's the last person I thought would be the calmest in this situation. But she is.

"Are you sure you're okay?" Courtney asks me. She touches my face gently, and then she's looking into my eyes. "Did you hit your head?"

I reach up, touch my head. Did I? I can't think. "I don't know."

I lean against her, shaking. I can't stop shaking, even though he's gone—because has he really gone? What if he's just outside?

She holds me tightly. "It'll be okay."

The police search the building and verify that Adam has gone. An officer takes statements from us all. Zara got most of it on camera. The police promise us all we'll be safe here now, but I can't sleep here tonight, I know that.

"You can stay at mine," Courtney says immediately, and I nod.

I lean against her. She's about the only thing that's keeping me upright.

Once the police have finished talking to us all, Zara and Zoe leave, and Courtney and I head to her apartment.

"I'd better phone Victoria and Martin. Let them know what's happened," I say as Courtney unlocks her door. "God, I feel so stupid. I didn't even have the door locked. And all this time, I've been worried about him coming in."

"We were filming though—so of course the door would be unlocked. It wasn't a normal day." Courtney gives me a small smile.

We sit on her sofa and she asks if I'm hungry. I shake my head. I'm too on edge to eat now.

Sergeant jumps up onto the sofa with us, settles at Courtney's side.

"It will be okay," she says, looking at me. She squeezes my hand. Then she looks down, and it's like she realizes what she's done. That it was fine to comfort me upstairs when Adam was there, and then when he'd gone and the police and Zara and Zoe were there—but not *here*. Because in her apartment, this feels different. This feels more intimate.

And we're alone.

She pulls her hand away, and immediately, coldness washes over me. Like without her touch, I'll never be warm again.

Sergeant stands and starts kneading the sofa cushion.

I turn to face her, get ready to speak, but she holds her hand up in a stop sign.

"I'm so sorry," Courtney says, her voice low and cracking. "About everything. I should've told you as soon as I realized, especially when we…" She trails off.

"It's… I'm sorry too." I reach for her hand. She hesitates for a moment, but then places hers in mine. "I… I'm guessing you've heard the cult rumors by now?" I wince.

She nods.

I squeeze her fingers tightly—and it feels good to touch her. To know she's solid, here, with me. "I… I'll explain everything to Victoria, okay? I'll make everything right."

She smiles, and it sounds like such a cliché, but her smile just lights me up. It makes me think that we *can* be something, that we *have* got a connection. Because her smile makes me feel alive.

"Do you think we can…" I look down at our hands. "…start again with all this?"

"Again?" She snorts. "I'm not redoing St. Bridget's."

I laugh. "Just the last few month or so then?"

The light in her eyes intensifies somehow, and she nods.

Relief pours through me, and I want to cry. Cry because she's here and I'm here, and this is it. "It's always been you," I say, squeezing her hand. "I can see that now."

FORTY-TWO

Courtney

One Year Later

WATERSTONES IS CROWDED, and it takes me a good few minutes to find Zara and Zoe and Dylan. They've claimed the romance corner and are talking excitedly. Zara sees me and waves me over.

"Hey!" I smile. "Wow, never expected it to be this busy." I twist around—from here, you can't even see the signing area where Sophie currently is.

My heart swells with pride. Her first book signing as a bestseller. And it's with that book—the one that now features me.

Catching Courtney didn't become a bestseller overnight, but six months ago, Zara's film won an inter-university award and then some clips of it were shared on Facebook and TikTok. A reporter then wrote an article specifically on Sophie's book prank, and linked to the book—and suddenly, boom, it was selling. And selling fast.

Sophie signed with an agent, and he got her a deal with one

of the big five for the same book—unusual, for a self-published book, Sophie said. But this just proves how good her book is. The publisher gave it the new title—*Catching Courtney*—and poured a load of marketing support into it.

And I look around the shop—people are going mad for it. Sophie's only doing signings across Devon and Cornwall, and so many of these people are clutching suitcases, like they just got off the train.

I catch sight of Mrs. Dalton, and my heart speeds up a little. She sees me and gives me a nod. Things still aren't normal between the two of us, and, to be honest, I doubt they ever will be. But she's trying, and it means a lot to Sophie if the two of us are civil.

"And how does it feel to know you're the lucky fan going home with the author?" Zara puts on a low voice, and then starts laughing.

"Seriously?" I smirk.

"What? It's what all the reporters say at award nights, right? This is the equivalent."

"Shhh," Dylan says, stretching onto his tiptoes so he can see over the crowd. "I think she's about to give her speech now."

"Not the speech," Zoe mutters, rolling her eyes.

We've all heard numerous versions of this speech for the last few weeks. I feel like I could give the speech myself.

We move forward as a group and somehow manage to squeeze around the side of the crowd, until we can see her.

Sophie starts by thanking her agent and editor, and everyone at the publishing house who worked on the book. She talks about the revisions they all made to the story, and then she goes on to thank all her readers.

"And, finally, I'd like to thank my girlfriend," Sophie says, and suddenly my heart is beating way too fast. "There she is—Courtney. Yes, I know you've all heard the story of how she came to be in this book. But I just want to thank you, Courtney. Because none of this would've been possible without you. Plus, I'm really glad you didn't sue me."

Laughter rumbles across the room, but only part of me notices, because the rest of me is focused on Sophie. How comfortable she looks up there. She's got that spark in her eye again—the spark she had at school. Only now it's slightly different too. She's calmer. But she's got confidence.

And, in this moment, watching my partner up there, I've never felt happier.

Acknowledgments

As always, writing this book hasn't been a solitary process. So many people have helped me with *It's Always Been You*, and I'm so grateful to you all.

To Sarah Anderson—thank you so much for all your editorial insight, and for helping me brainstorm some of the pranks in this book! I had so much fun chatting to you about this, and your enthusiasm really lifted me.

To my authenticity and sensitivity readers, Jack Ori and Jude Kamler: thank you so much for your invaluable feedback on this manuscript and its portrayal of the ace trans characters. Any mistakes or errors are mine.

To my beta-readers: Celeste Hannah, Tracey Dunn McDermott, Mariana Rodrigues, Linda Izquierdo Ross, Saffron Long, and Lori Backner. Thank you for taking the time to read early drafts of this book and giving me feedback which ultimately helped me shape this into something I'm so proud of.

To Sarah Anderson (again!)—thank you for the gorgeous design work you did for this book. The cover is simply perfect! You've really made my story come to life.

To my writing cheerleaders: Emily Colin, Lisa Amowitz, and Heidi Ayarbe, thank you so much for always being supportive.

To my parents and my brother: thank you so much for everything.

And to Michael: thank you for your endless encouragement.

About the Author

Elin Annalise writes contemporary novels featuring asexual characters. She graduated from Exeter University in 2016, where she studied English literature and watched the baby rabbits play on the lawns when she should've been taking notes on Milton and Homer. She's a big fan of koi carp, cats, and dreaming.

Elin's books include *In My Dreams*, *My Heart to Find*, and *It's Always Been You.*

Lightning Source UK Ltd.
Milton Keynes UK
UKHW010133130522
402932UK00001B/188